Gone . . .

Gone . . .

Debbie S. Blankenship

RESOURCE *Publications* · Eugene, Oregon

GONE . . .

Resource Publications
An Imprint of Wipf and Stock Publishers
199 W. 8th Ave., Suite 3
Eugene, OR 97401

www.wipfandstock.com

PAPERBACK ISBN: 978-1-6667-3817-9
HARDCOVER ISBN: 978-1-6667-9852-4
EBOOK ISBN: 978-1-6667-9853-1

MARCH 9, 2022 10:04 AM

I could not have written this book without the help of my dear friend Dottie Reinke. She was my sounding board, my critic, my editor, and my biggest cheerleader. When I didn't know how to start, she gave me great ideas.

Without her friendship I could very well still be a lost soul wandering this earth. Thank you for friending that weird girl that sat next to you in Jr High music class.

I also want to thank my good friend Cindy Odneal for her help with the final editing of this book. I couldn't have done it without you!

Contents

J OHN BLAKELY dreams of reporting the *big story*, but when he finally gets the assignment to find out why people have gone missing, it hits a little too close to home. He soon discovers the dangers of this new world while trying to figure out what happened. His ensuing journey leads him to faith, and, ultimately, the family he always dreamed of.

Chapter 1

Gone . . .

S OMETHING had just happened in the tower. There was a noise, a shout or a horn blast, a movement of some kind, and 16 of the 50 air traffic controllers were gone. Just gone! Everyone in the room scrambled to try to monitor the planes left unattended. As they watched in horror, some of the planes began to descend, with calls to the pilot unanswered. Frantic calls from other planes were reporting missing pilots or co-pilots, missing passengers, missing attendants. Sasha frantically tried to contact the two planes that were drifting into each other's flight path. One of the flight attendants on flight 842 came on the radio, frantically calling for help, reporting no pilots on board. Sasha hollered for Steve, who was a pilot, to take over for flight 842 and help the attendant change course. Steve's voice came on the radio, trying to get instructions to the attendant, but it wasn't in time, and both planes disappeared from their screens . . .

On flight 842, Shaun, the flight attendant, was pushing his cart down the aisle, serving drinks to the passengers. He thought he heard something and looked back towards the cockpit. Suddenly passengers were screaming and when he turned to face the man he had just served, he was gone! The woman seated next to him was also gone, and the young woman that was seated next to the window was screaming. Several of the other passengers were also screaming, getting out of their seats, looking for someone. He hollered for everyone to sit back down and put on their seat belts, and quickly pushed his cart back to its station. Knocking on the cockpit door, he was going to inform the pilot to turn back, something was wrong. The door flew open and another attendant screamed at him that the pilots had disappeared! He stared in disbelief at the two empty seats; no one was flying the plane! He got in the pilot's chair and tried to radio the tower, but there was no response. Frantically he grabbed the controls as the plane started to descend. Finally, a voice came over the radio and he screamed into it, "We don't have any pilots! What should I do?" Sasha told him to stay calm, she would find someone to help him. A minute later he was on the radio with Steve, who was trying to give him instructions on how to correct their course. Suddenly another plane came into view just beneath them. Shaun tried to pull up, but realized he was not going to miss the other plane. He locked eyes with the other attendant . . .

Pat, the shift supervisor at the nuclear plant, was checking the pressure gauges with Ron when he heard a strange noise and looked back towards the door. Seeing nothing there, he turned back to the controls saying, "We need to go check the other gauges", when he realized Ron was no longer beside him. Pat went to the main control room, thinking that was where Ron had gone, but he was not there either. Just then an alarm started to sound and another employee came running up to him screaming about people disappearing from their posts, leaving vital controls unattended. They had been having trouble with some of the release valves and Pat stared in horror as gauges began to fluctuate with no one to correct the pressures. He tried to make the corrections himself, but couldn't get the valves to release together like they should. The building began to shudder under the increasing pressure. Pat hit the evacuation alarm and everyone began running out of the facility . . .

Adam was grumbling as he drove his 18-wheeler through Chicago's rush hour traffic. He had hoped to make it through there much earlier, but construction had slowed his progress. His radio was playing loudly, but he thought he heard a horn and looked in his rear-view mirror. Suddenly, a car swerved into his lane directly in front of him. He slammed on his brakes, barely missing the car. As he watched the car drift into the next lane, he realized several cars and trucks in front of him were crashing into each other. There was no way to avoid them. He closed his eyes, bracing for impact . . .

I sat in my car, stunned by what just happened. A large dump truck had narrowly missed me as it cascaded down a hill into the front of someone's house, spilling its load of gravel as it smashed through the brick wall. I pulled over, watching other cars crashing into each other. "Elle, you're not going to believe this!" I said into my phone. "There are cars crashing into each other everywhere!"

There was silence on the other end.

"Elle? Are you still there?"

Wondering if I had accidentally hung up, I checked the second counter on my phone. It showed the call was still connected.

"Hello, Elle?"

There was no response, so I hung up.

I got out of my car to see if anyone needed help as I dialed 911. The line was busy, so I hung up and went to check on the truck driver that had hit the house.

"Is everyone OK?" I asked as the family came outside.

"Yes, fortunately no one was in that bedroom at the time!" a woman replied.

We all rushed over to the truck, looking inside for the driver, but no one was there.

"Did you see him get out?" the woman asked.

"No, I didn't see anyone," I replied, looking around the truck.

Someone started screaming down the street, so I ran over to see what happened. A young woman was hysterically searching for her sister. When I got her to calm down, she told me she was riding with her sister, Mary, to work when she suddenly disappeared.

"I tried to grab the steering wheel, but couldn't reach the brakes and we crashed into the car beside us! Then we were hit from behind and ran into the telephone pole!"

She was sobbing as I tried to console her. She seemed physically ok, so I told her help was on the way and went to the other car that was crashed near her. There was an elderly man behind the steering wheel. He was slumped over, not moving. I checked his pulse, but couldn't find one. Emergency sirens started filling the air. The sidewalks and streets became crowded with people who all seemed to be frantically searching for someone.

I went back to my car and tried Elle again, but the line was busy. I needed to get to her coffee shop to be sure she was ok. I managed to drive a few blocks, but many of the roads were completely blocked with accidents. The news station that I had been listening to was reporting that people had disappeared, causing nationwide chaos. My heart began to pound faster as I wondered what happened, especially to Elle. After turning down several unfamiliar streets looking for a clear lane to drive down, I couldn't go any farther, so I pulled over as best I could and went on foot. Again, I tried to call Elle and this time it rang, but then went to her voicemail.

It was like the city had gone crazy. Cars all over the roads, people wandering the streets calling out names, crying, shaking. I didn't know what was happening. I picked up my pace a little, thinking there must be a better way to get across town. Now I was wishing I had relied a little less on the Maps app.

Then I spotted a familiar face from the office staff at the TV station.

"Sharon!" I hollered. "Sharon!"

She was frantically searching for someone, so I ran across the street.

"Sharon, are you ok?"

I put my hand on her arm and she turned to me with a look of terror.

"I can't find Owen," she cried. "He was just here!"

I looked around. There were no children in sight. "Owen? Your little boy?"

"Yes! He was just out in the yard with his friends!" she sobbed. "We can't find any of them! They're gone!"

"Gone? What do you mean?"

I wanted answers, but she was joined by a group of parents and they all ran off in another direction yelling for their kids. Panic started to grip my heart. What is going on? Just then a large plane flew low over our heads, headed east. I watched as it disappeared on the horizon behind the trees and buildings. I kept searching the sky to see if it had pulled up, but then I saw a big black smoke cloud and heard the crash. I estimated it had made it just over the river.

Now I started running. Could it be another terrorist attack? I dodged people, jumped over abandoned backpacks, purses, and briefcases. Clearly people had really vanished suddenly, leaving their personal belongings behind. How could terrorists make people disappear? I tried to call Elle again, but the line was busy, then there was no service.

As I ran, my mind went back to the first time I met Elle. She was a new owner of a local coffee shop where I often stopped, too many times in a day, to keep myself going through a sometimes boring schedule. As a new reporter, I was assigned the 'filler pieces', some (really most) never even making it on the ½ hour newscast. She was always there, trying to keep her shop alive. The pandemic and following worker shortage made it difficult. I admired her tenacity; she was determined not to quit. She would greet me with, "Hey John, high octane today?" and it made me laugh every time. We started to have small conversations at first, chit chat mostly, but gradually we started sharing our stories. I found out she had graduated with a degree in business just last year. She had come into some inheritance money and was trying to decide what to do with it and her career. I smiled a little as I remembered how she had told me she felt God was giving her direction . . . leading her to purchase the coffee shop. How she had dismissed the idea several times, only to have it come back to her, stronger each time. I remembered rolling my eyes a little when she talked about God "leading" her. She said she finally thought, *Ok Lord, if this is where you want me, ok.*

I was jolted back to reality when I hit the ground. Someone had run into me . . . or had I run into them? I wasn't sure. As I caught my breath, I took in the scene around me. Has the world gone mad? People weeping, people running, some looked shell shocked. A mob was starting to form and I watched as they broke into a Radio Barn and started looting. I got up and tried to get my bearings when something struck my head . . . and I felt myself falling again . . .

I was back in the coffee shop, watching Elle make a customer her usual. When she left, Elle walked over and smiled. I loved that smile. In truth, I was falling in love with her, but hadn't admitted it to myself. She was not like any girl I had known, so open and caring. There weren't the usual phony games I had played with other girls, not that there had been that many women in my life. I really was pretty shy. My mom died when I was nine and my dad . . . well, I didn't want to go there.

"Where are you off to today?" Elle asked.

I chuckled a little, "A big story today! Some campers claim they saw Bigfoot!"

We both laughed.

"Someday you will get that big story, John. Don't be discouraged."

Always the optimist.

"How is business?" I asked.

"Oh, it's going to turn the corner any day! Soon I'll be able to afford to drink my own coffee!"

We laughed again.

"I'm trusting God will provid; He always does."

I cocked my head. When Elle said things like this, I was always a little intrigued. Trusting God was something I couldn't figure out. I remembered my mom used to take me to church when I was small. I didn't remember much about it, except maybe the Sunday school teacher. She was a nice lady and used to give us cookies while she taught Bible stories about giants and floods. After my mom died, I was left alone with my father . . . God was not in my life anymore.

I became aware of voices around me and forced my eyes open. My head was pounding. What happened? I looked around, blinking, trying to focus.

"Hey man, you ok?"

I knew that voice. "Danny? Is that you? What happened?"

"Don't get up," Danny cautioned. "You have a nasty bump on your head. We saw you get hit with a brick. A couple of us ran out and dragged you in here."

My head was still pounding, but my eyes seemed to be focusing now. I looked around and realized I was in a small church with a few other people. They were sitting together in the wooden pews discussing something. A young woman had a Bible in her hands and was reading it.

Elle . . . I suddenly remembered.

"Danny, I was talking to Elle just before the phones went dead. Have you seen her?" Danny starred at me for a minute.

"No, I haven't seen her."

Danny was Elle's younger brother. He worked in her shop sometimes. That's how I got to know him.

"I've got to get over there. I'm a little turned around. Can you help me?" I begged. Danny looked at the floor, then at the group of people still sitting in the pews.

"Yeah, I can get you over there. You better go in the bathroom and get cleaned up first."

"Do I look that bad?" I asked, trying to smile.

He helped me up and showed me where the bathrooms were, then went over to the small group of people. I went in and looked in the mirror. My right eye was swollen and there was blood running down the side of my head. I took some paper towels and wiped the blood off. The scene gave me a flashback and I was suddenly back in junior high and my father was screaming at me. I tried apologizing for whatever it was he was mad about, when his fisted hand slammed into the side of my head. I fell to the floor, covering my head, trying to stop any further blows to my face.

Danny knocked and looked in.

"You ok?"

That pulled me back into reality, and I answered, "Yeah, I'll be ready in a minute."

CHAPTER 2

My Big Story

THE scene outside was chaos. It looked like every person in the city was wandering around, crying, searching, screaming. Mobs continued to form, and homes and businesses were being broken into and emptied. As Danny led me along, I noticed some business owners were standing outside with loaded guns, threatening anyone who approached. We didn't talk. I don't think either of us had any words, just total disbelief of what was happening.

I finally recognized where we were and ran ahead to the shop. I burst through the door, yelling for Elle. It looked empty. Danny came in behind me.

"Elle! I yelled again. I went around the counter and found the cash register open and emptied of all cash. I looked at Danny.

"What do you think happened?"

He stood there, silent. I ran up the stairs to Elle's little apartment over the shop calling her name, but there was no one there.

"She's not up there!" I shouted, and as I walked back around the counter, I stepped on something. It was Elle's phone! Now I was sure something had happened to her. She wouldn't have left her phone there, even if it was dead.

"Danny, we have to keep looking for her!" I yelled, as I made my way back to the door. He just stood there.

"Danny, come on!" I hollered again.

He started to laugh, almost hysterically. He picked up a cup and threw it across the room.

"Don't you get it?" he screamed. "She's gone!"

"I know!" I yelled back. "Why are you just standing there? Let's go!!"

Danny's laughing turned into weeping.

He's really losing it . . .

"She was right," he muttered. "She was right," he repeated louder. "It's true, it's all true . . . . God forgive me, she was right," and he ran out the door.

What the . . . I ran out after him, but lost him in the crowd. I just stood there, searching the streets, more confused than ever. What the hell was he talking about?

Just then my phone went off. It was my boss.

"Blakely," I said.

"Well, at least you're still here. Get in the office, now!"

"Yes sir, I'll be there in a minute," and took off running towards the station. It wasn't far from the coffee shop, so I got there quickly. Surely they would know what happened.

The scene in the office was almost as chaotic as out on the street. Several of the reporters could not be reached and Charlie, my boss, was barking orders at everyone. He looked at me.

"What happened to you? You look terrible!"

"Long story."

"Airways are still down," he barked. "We can't get in touch with some of our staff. I want you out on the streets getting interviews! See if anyone knows what's going on, if they saw or heard anything. People have disappeared and I want to know why! I can't give you a camera guy; you'll have to do it yourself."

He practically threw me the camera. I started to ask a question, but he motioned for me to get going. *This is ridiculous, I don't know if I can even run this thing,* but I went back out the door.

A thought ran through my mind; *Elle, I think I just got that big story.*

I couldn't let myself think about her right now. Maybe I would run into her on the street . . . I found a group of guys standing on the corner outside the Main Street Pub. They were watching the activity on the block, so I approached them and asked if I could interview them. They said sure so I set up the camera on the tripod and turned it on.

"This is John Blakely with KWZZ news. Who am I talking with?" I held the mic out to the closest man.

"Berry Sims" he answered.

"Berry, did you see or hear anything this morning before people started to disappear?" I pushed the mic at him again.

He leaned toward it, "Yes, I heard this weird scuffling noise in the apartment next to me. When I knocked on the door, no one answered. It was unlocked so I opened it and called out, but the apartment was empty. The table was set, and coffee poured, but they were gone!"

"Do you know who lived there?" I asked.

"It was an older couple, Max and Jo. I think they were retired. Max drove a school bus. Jo, her health wasn't great, but she would make me cookies once in a while."

"Do you have any theories as to what happened?" I held the mic in front of another man's face.

"We were just trying to figure that out. Could it be aliens?" He was nearly whispering and looking behind me as if watching for someone.

I turned the mic toward another guy's face. "Is that what you think, aliens?"

He shrugged. "Sure, why not? People have been getting abducted by aliens for years. This time they weren't messing around."

He kept talking but I took the mic away, thanked them and looked for someone else, anyone else, to interview. Really, my big story is aliens?!?! Could that be real??

There must be someone with a better idea. Walking a little further down the street, I came upon a car wreck with some EMT workers. I went up to them to see if I could get their take on what had happened. They had a body on a stretcher and were getting ready to walk it out since they could not get their ambulance onto the street. The body was covered, so I assumed the person had not survived the crash. I didn't have time to set up my camera, so I just used my phone to record.

"Excuse me, John Blakely from KWZZ News. What have you been told about the cause of these accidents?" I asked the rescue worker closest to me.

She just shook her head. "All I know is people are reporting accidents with vehicles that don't have drivers. The drivers are just gone! There are so many abandoned cars we can't get to the crash sites. I've never seen anything like it."

I stopped and let them do their job, recording part of their effort. I kept walking, and then realized I was back in front of the coffee shop. I fought back tears, trying not to fall apart. "Keep it together man!" I said out loud. "Just do your job!"

There was a group of middle-aged people sitting on a porch just down the road. They looked approachable, so I walked up to the group.

"Do you mind if I interview you on camera?" I asked. They all agreed, so I set up my camera again.

"This is John Blakely from KWZZ news. Who are you sir?"

"Bob Smither."

"Do you have any ideas as to what happened this morning?"

"Yes sir, we know exactly what happened. We've been predicting it for months now," he said confidently.

"And what is that?" I asked.

The man turned directly toward the camera and shouted, "Why do you think the government was pushing those Covid vaccines so hard? Population control! If you were stupid enough to get the shot, then it was bye bye to you!"

I bit my lip a little.

"So, you think somehow the government made all these people disappear?"

"You bet! NASA, CIA, FBI, all those secret government agencies . . . who knows what they have been working on!"

I asked the others with Bob if they agreed and some nodded enthusiastically, while others shrugged.

"Ok, thank you for your time," I said as I started to take the camera down.

One of them asked, "What do you think happened?"

I didn't have a good answer so just smiled and said, "That's what I'm trying to figure out."

I couldn't take another conspiracy theory, so I walked back to the coffee shop and went in. I sat down at my usual table, half expecting Elle to come over with my usual order. I couldn't process this. I'm not a praying man. In fact, I'm not sure I believe in God, but the only words that came to me were, "God, what is happening?"

Suddenly, a guy in a dark hoodie came bursting through the door. He saw me sitting there with an expensive camera and pulled a knife. I stood up slowly and said, "Wait a minute, calm down," holding my hands up trying to show him I didn't want a fight. He walked over to the register and saw it open and empty.

Pointing the knife towards me he yelled, "Back away from the table!"

"Look buddy, the camera isn't mine. I have to return it to the station. Why don't you just move on?"

"Give me your wallet!" he barked. With one hand I slowly reached for my wallet and set it on the table. As he came over to get it, something in me just snapped. With everything else that was happening today, I was not going to get robbed!! I lunged for him, grabbing the knife hand. We were in a struggle that I soon realized could be life or death for one of us. We were both trying to get control of the knife. He was stronger than I thought. I had his arm and he had mine. We were locked in a wrestling match. I used every ounce of my strength to push him backwards a little. He started to fall, and I lost my hold on the knife hand. I felt the blade slice through the skin on my arm. With my last bit of strength, I pushed him backwards and he fell over a chair. I backed away, trying to regroup, when he grabbed the camera and ran out the door.

"Shit!" *How am going to explain this!*

I reached down to get my wallet that had fallen off the table during the scuffle. At least he didn't take that. Blood was running down my arm. It was a nasty cut, but didn't look life threatening. I wrapped a bar towel around it to stop the bleeding. It was starting to throb. I sat back down and kept pressure on the wound. I was shaking all over from the adrenaline rush and I thought, *Here's my big story Elle, man assaulted in local coffee shop.*

I started to laugh, like a crazy person, hysterically, and then I was weeping with my head in my hands. I was glad you weren't there to see me . . . and yet I wished with every fiber of my being that you were.

CHAPTER 3

Meet the Cat

I SAT there a long time, lost in my memories. Finally, I got up and headed back to the station.

"The boss is going to love this, no usable stories and no camera," I said out loud. I barely noticed what was happening on the street as I walked. I got to the station and went in. The crew was getting ready to broadcast.

Good. Maybe we'll get some information if the stations are up and running again.

Charlie came up to me. "You look like you were hit by a bus . . . you weren't, were you?"

"Not a bus, but some guy with a knife now has your camera."

He looked at my arm and the blood-soaked towel. "You better go have that looked at. Do you need a ride to the emergency room?"

"No, I can get there, it's not far."

He shook his head. "Take the rest of the day. But I need you back on the streets tomorrow!"

"Yes sir." I nodded and started to leave.

"John!" he called. "Did you hear anything that makes sense?"

"No, just conspiracy theories and aliens."

He sighed and nodded as he turned away.

I must really look bad—he didn't even yell about the camera.

I made my way to the emergency room. They were triaging people before they let them in the door. Some cots were lined up outside with people on them, waiting their turns to get in. Towards the back side of the hospital, I also noticed lines of body bags.

A nurse came over and unwrapped my arm. It was still bleeding some.

"You're going to need some stitches in that. Wait here while I see if we have a doctor that can help you."

I nodded my head. I wasn't feeling too great. All the excitement of the day and blood loss was catching up with me. She was back in a few minutes with another nurse who led me inside to a small room.

She examined my arm and said, "That's a pretty deep cut. I'm afraid you'll need several stitches. When was the last time you had a tetanus shot?"

"I think maybe high school?"

She took my insurance card and said she would be back in a minute. She came back with a doctor who cleaned and stitched up my arm. Then the nurse wrapped it back up, and gave me instructions to keep it clean, yada yada, and sent me home. I was supposed to go to my primary physician in a couple weeks to get the stitches out. Then she added that if I couldn't find him, to just come back here. Our eyes locked for a few seconds, with unspoken panic passing between us. Who knew what the next two weeks would bring . . .

As I left the hospital it dawned on me, *I have no way to get home.* At least my phone had service. I could use my GPS to get home, but I was physically and mentally exhausted. I looked at my Uber app . . . . What the heck; I called it. No answer. I punched in 'home' on my Maps app for walking directions. Four hours . . . . I was laughing hysterically again. Could this day get any better??

I headed back to the coffee shop. I would crash in Elle's apartment for the night. When I got there, I realized I hadn't eaten anything all day. I scrounged around looking for scones or muffins. The place was pretty ransacked. I started to go upstairs, then stopped. What if someone was up there? The last thing I needed was another fight. I went back down to the coffee bar looking for a weapon of some kind. I found a sharp knife in a drawer and quietly headed back upstairs. I tried the door at the top; it clicked open. The sun was starting to set but there was just enough light for me to see in the room. It looked clean; no one had ransacked it. *Good.* I flipped on the light and listened for any sound of movement. Nothing. I began to relax. I shut the door at the top of the stairs and locked it. Then I placed a kitchen chair under the doorknob like I'd seen in the movies. I set the knife on the table next to the sofa, just in case. I was hungry, thirsty, and exhausted. I laid down on the sofa and passed out. The night was filled with bizarre dreams of people disappearing, turning into ash, and floating away in the wind. Dreams of Elle and I, walking along the riverbank, watching the sunset.

I slowly began to realize there was something on me, I could feel it's movement on my chest. Then something wet touched my chin. I jolted awake, trying to throw it off while groping for the knife on the table. I fell off the couch, crashing into the coffee table, still groping for the knife. Whatever was on me ran off into the kitchen with lots of growling and hissing.

The cat . . . I had forgotten Elle had a cat. Somewhere between relief and anger, I got up off the floor. Woah, I sat back down. My head and arm were throbbing, and the room was spinning. I leaned back, trying to relax. I needed some water . . . and some ibuprofen. When the room stopped spinning, I slowly got back up and walked into the kitchen.

"Where would she keep the meds?" I said out loud and pulled all the cabinets open. I found some pill bottles . . . Yes! Ibuprofen! I poured four out in my hand, took a glass out and filled it with water. I downed it and filled it again. Elle's phone charger was on the counter, so I plugged in mine for a quick charge. I had to eat something, so I continued pulling the cabinets open. Cereal, peanut butter, bread, I pulled it all out. Anything and everything looked good. PB and J never tasted so good!

After my 'feast' I sat back down on the couch. Muffin peeked around the corner at me.

"Here kitty. Sorry I scared you. Come here."

She slowly walked over and rubbed on my leg.

"I bet you're hungry. Let's see if I can find you some food."

I went back to the kitchen and searched the cabinets again for cat food.

"Here it is!"

I shook the bag at Muffin who promptly ran over to her bowls. I filled one bowl as full as I could get it, then filled the other with water.

"That should hold you for a little while." I felt my strength returning.

"What is your plan, John?" I said to myself. "I need a plan." I'll hit the streets again, see if I can get some audio on my phone.

First, I better clean up, I thought, as I walked into the bathroom. My eye was a bright purple and swollen even more than it was yesterday. I pushed memories of my father out of my mind as I washed up and steered them back to what Danny had said the last time I saw him. What was Elle 'right' about? What was 'true'? I needed to find Danny, but where to start? I didn't know where he lived. Where was that little church again? There was a Radio Barn near it. I pulled my phone off the charger and typed in 'Radio Barn near me'. My phone pulled up several. Ok, well, I'll start with the nearest one going back towards my house. I also needed to get back to my car.

Before I left the apartment, I turned on the TV. The emergency broadcast system had been activated on all the channels, telling people where to tune in for news. I found the station and listened. The disappearances were global. They were telling people to shelter in place and there was a 6:00 pm curfew. No exceptions; arrests would be made. The National Guard and the Army were called out nationwide. If you were missing a family member you were supposed to call the 800 number provided and leave a report. Electricity outages were reported across the country. If you worked for an electric company, you were to report to the office. If you were an electrician, police officer, or hospital staff, you were also supposed to report to work. Abandoned cars would be towed away.

That was all the news I could handle, so I turned it off. I knew I needed to get to my car before they towed it, so I grabbed my phone and a water bottle. I locked the apartment door. There were some other keys on here, maybe they locked the coffee shop door. Sure enough, they did, so I locked it up too, hoping I wouldn't come back to broken windows. Just as I was locking the door a police car pulled up and turned his lights on. He got out of the car and said "Sir, keep your hands where I can see them." He had his hand on his gun. For a second, I wondered who he was talking to, then realized it was me. I put my hands up. "Turn around and keep your hands on the building" he said. I complied. He patted me down and when he was confident that I didn't have a weapon told me to turn around.

"Do you have any ID?" he asked.

"Yes sir." I slowly reached for my wallet and pulled out my driver's license. I also handed him my ID from the station. He went back to his car and ran them on his computer.

"What are you doing here?" he asked, as he handed me back my ID.

"I was looking for my friend. She owns this shop and I was locking it up. It's already been robbed though. Her name is Elle Murphy. Do you have any information on her?"

"You'll have to call the hotline to report any missing persons," he replied.

"I had to abandon my car yesterday. Could you tell me if it's been towed? I was just going to walk back over there to get it."

He studied me for a second.

"What are the plates? I can see if it's in the system yet."

I gave him the plates and he went back to his car.

Maybe I look bad enough that he feels sorry for me.

He came back and said it was not in the system yet, so there was a good chance it had not been towed.

"Where did you leave it?" he asked me.

"Over on Elm, near Ivy Street. The road was blocked yester-day. I tried to pull it out of the way when I left it."

"I can give you a ride over there; you look like you could use one," he said.

"Thanks!"

I got in the car and we road quietly for a few blocks.

"How did you get the black eye?" he asked me.

"I was on the wrong end of a brick yesterday."

"I've been there before," he looked at me and smiled a little.

I nodded my head, "I don't know how you do it. I have a lot of respect for law enforcement. Do you know what happened?"

"A lot of people disappeared," was all he said.

The roads were pretty clear, so it didn't take us long to get to my car. He dropped me off and said, "Pay attention to that curfew."

"I will officer, thank you for the lift," and he drove off.

CHAPTER 4

The Letter

M Y car looked ok. I unlocked it and got in. A wave of emotions flooded me. Just a day ago life was normal . . . good even. How did this happen!? I couldn't stop the tears. *Come on, John, pull it together!* I pushed my emotions back down inside of me. *Concentrate!* With a big sigh, I turned the key. Trying to remember which route I walked, I drove slowly away. My phone still had Radio Barn pulled up, so I started a route to one, realized I was going in the wrong direction, then 'recalculated' to another. This looked right. As I came up to the store, I scanned the area for a church. Yes! It was just a block over. I pulled up in front and went to the door, but it was locked. I knocked, but no one answered. Disappointment covered me. My mind was scrambling for another plan, but didn't have one. I just sat down on the steps.

It was then that I noticed a woman coming out of the Radio Barn with a cart full of stuff. I decided to go over to interview her. I grabbed my cell phone and started to record.

"Hi, I'm John Blakely from KWZZ. Could I ask you some questions?"

She eyed me suspiciously and kept on walking.

"Can you tell me why you need batteries, and a solar radio? What do you think is going on?" I asked as I walked with her.

"If you're smart you will do the same thing, before it's too late," she answered.

"Too late for what?" I was puzzled.

"We are under attack and you better find a bunker or somewhere to live," she replied.

"Under attack? Who do you think is attacking us?" I hoped she wouldn't say aliens.

"We're not sure yet, but it's pretty obvious, isn't it?" She paused for a second to make eye contact with me.

"We? So there are others who believe this? Are they all living in bunkers?" I questioned.

She avoided my question. "It's not going to get any better; you need to prepare." With that she got in her car and drove off.

Well, it's as good a guess as any.

I walked back over to the church and knocked one more time. This time someone opened the door. "John?" It was Danny. I walked over and gave him a big hug. He didn't even act like that was weird, though it was, kind of. We had not been close, just casual acquaintances, really. But he hugged me back.

"I'm so glad I found you!"

Backing up, he eyed me up and down. "You look terrible," he joked.

I laughed. "Can I talk to you for a minute?"

"Of course!" and he led me to the back room. I noticed that same small group of people were still there.

"We can't bring ourselves to leave," Danny said when he saw me looking at the others. "There's a comfort being here." We sat down in the small office.

"Danny, what did you mean when you said, 'she was right?'" I blurted out the question.

He studied my face, then said, "Do you remember how Elle would speak of her faith?"

I nodded.

"We grew up in the church. She believed, but I . . . I was stubborn and rebellious and wrote God and Jesus off as a crutch that some people needed to get through the day."

"Ok, but . . . " I started to say.

Danny held up his hand. "Just let me finish before you say anything. This is all new to me. Elle would talk about the end times, about when Jesus was going to come and take his believers. I believe that is what happened." He stopped to look me in the eyes. "I know, sounds kind of crazy, but it's the best explanation for what is happening."

I stared at him, trying to read his eyes. He was absolutely serious.

"Look Danny, I can see you're serious, but I really don't know what you're talking about."

"The rapture. It's all in the Bible," he went on. "I never believed it was real, but we've been reading it together (motioning towards the others), and it all fits. How could it be so accurate if it's not true?"

Could he be right?

"John, come and talk with the others."

I wasn't ready to listen to them. "Maybe another time Danny; I should probably get back to work," and I left.

"Really God? Was this you?" I said out loud.

My phone went off. It was a text from my boss.

"Sorry," I texted back. "I was going to let you know that I was following up on some leads."

He said that was fine. I thought about going home, but wound up back at the coffee shop. It was like I didn't know where else to go. The shop looked fine; no broken windows. I went in and locked the door behind me. *Just in case . . .*

The coffee smelled so good. *Could I run this thing?* I wondered. I had watched Elle many times, but never with the idea that I'd be making my own someday. It looked like the power was on, so I flipped a switch. Hot water came pouring out.

"Oops! I guess I need some coffee in there." I found the right parts and added the coffee the way Elle had. "It worked!" I took a large cup upstairs with me. I stood in the apartment; just stood there. I didn't know what to think or to feel. I hadn't felt this lost since my mom died.

Elle's computer was over on a table in the corner. I could use that to type up some of the opinions I'd gotten. I walked over to it and opened it. It opened to her email and a draft of a letter. 'Dear John', it began.

What!? I sat down and started reading it.

> Dear John,
>
> I've been wanting to talk with you for some time. I know we 'talk', but I want to explain some things to you. I've grown very fond of you over the past few months, too fond. And I think you are feeling the same thing, even though neither one of us has admitted it. I gave my life to Jesus a long time ago and have tried to live my life following Him. I know your childhood was hard and you never really had someone to show you what life with Christ could be. I'd love to talk to you about faith and answer any questions you might have. You have been on my heart a lot lately, like God is leading me to you. (I see the eye roll;) Please think about it and let me know if you want to talk.
>
> Love, Elle

Never sent . . . . She never got the chance to send it. My hands were shaking as I hit the send button. *We can never have this talk.* I would have come—I would have welcomed the talk. I *did* have questions. I knew she had something that I did not. An assurance, a hope . . . Muffin came over and rubbed my leg. I reached down to pet her, with tears forming in my eyes. I knew what I had to do. I got back in my car and drove to the church. I knocked on the door and Danny answered again. He looked at my face and knew, "Hey everyone, this is my good friend John . . . "

CHAPTER 5

The Good Samaritan

I HAD a lot to think about when I left that church. I drove back to the office to try to get something down on paper.

"John, what do you have for me?" Charlie always got right to the point.

"I've got several different opinions. Let me get them on my computer."

"Good" he said. "Send them to me as soon as you can."

I sat down at my desk. This felt good; almost normal.

Opinion 1- Aliens; the theory being instead of only abducting one person, they took a large sampling of the world's population.

Opinion 2- the government has used the Covid vaccinations to somehow trace and abduct people, for unclear motives. Possibly population control.

Opinion 3- Doomsday scenario; people living in bunkers or underground. The world under attack by unknown forces.

Opinion 4- The rapture, as predicted in the Bible. The return of Christ. All believers are taken to heaven in preparation for seven years of tribulation.

I supported these opinions with quotes from some of the people I had interviewed and the discussion at the church before I sent them over to my boss. "Which do I believe?" I asked myself. I didn't really have an answer yet.

I brought up the national news on my computer. The governments were trying to get a handle on the looting, but there just weren't enough police to handle it. Special forces were being brought in; Army forces, National guard units, SWAT teams. Several planes had crashed into large metropolitan areas as well as rural, and fires were burning uncontrolled. The nuclear reactor at Nine Mile Point in New York had suffered damage and was being monitored for radiation leaks. There was still a lot of panic on the streets. What was really disturbing was that all the small children had disappeared everywhere. Many entire families were gone without a trace. It was like we had been sucked into an episode of 'The Twilight Zone'. My phone buzzed; it was my boss wanting me to come to his office. As I walked in, I saw Katie, one of our camera persons, sitting there. I sat down next to her.

"John, I was just telling Katie that I want to send you two back out on the street to get some video coverage of what's happening locally."

"Ok." I looked at Katie, "Are you ready?"

"I will be in few minutes. I'll meet you in the equipment room."

I nodded as we walked out and went back to my office to grab some things. I dug around in my drawers for something to eat and found a couple protein bars. I shoved them in my pocket and grabbed a bottle of water. I was suddenly aware that I had been in my clothes for two days now . . . . I sniffed myself. *Oh well, it is what it is.*

When I got to the equipment room, Katie wasn't there, so I looked for a camera and made sure I had a fresh battery pack. She came in the room.

"I'm ready, did you get it all?"

"I think so."

We walked out to the parking garage and got into one of the station's vans.

"Any ideas where to start?" I asked.

"Why don't we just drive around and see what we can find."

Sounded like a plan, so I headed over towards the big stores to see if people were still looting. The streets were mostly clear. The abandoned vehicles that were blocking streets had been towed. There were still several on the side of the roads, but we could still get through. The government had instituted a 'no fly zone' over the whole country, so we didn't have anyone up in a helicopter to guide us.

"I hear you had a little trouble yesterday," she said as she looked me over.

"Oh yeah," I laughed. "It was quite a day".

"You can say that again," she replied soberly.

"Is your family still here?" I asked, and then almost immediately regretted it.

"I've talked to most of them," she replied, then looked out the side window and added, "No one has heard from my older sister. She moved to Wisconsin several years ago."

After a few minutes she asked, "How about your family?"

"I don't have any family," I lied. I hadn't talked to my dad since I was 18 and left the house.

We pulled up to a MegaMart super center. There were several cars in the parking lot and people were coming out with carts full of groceries and other items.

"Definitely looks like looters," she said. "Let's see if we can get some footage."

I pulled into the parking lot, but stayed toward the back with the stores behind me. Katie jumped out and started to unload the camera.

"I don't think we should stay too long," I said. "Things could get ugly."

We started the camera rolling. Katie decided to just hold it in case we needed to leave in a hurry.

I stepped in front of the camera. "This is John Blakely with KWZZ news. As you can see, the National Guard has not made it downtown yet. Looters continue to ravage the stores." I stepped aside so Katie could zoom in on what was happening. We watched as a young couple came out with a large cart full of items. As they got closer to their car, two men approached them and tried to get the cart away from the guy. He tried to fight them off, but they both turned on him and threw him onto the ground. His wife was screaming for help. I couldn't just stand there. I started to go over to help, but Katie grabbed my arm.

"Don't be stupid!" she yelled.

"Get in the van and start it up!" I yelled back. I ran over to the two guys who were now mercilessly hitting and kicking the man. I pulled one guy off and threw him down, then tried to grab the other guy. He came at me fists flying. I managed to duck the punch and grabbed him in a bear hug so he couldn't get any leverage for additional blows. The other guy was back up and coming at us. I shoved the guy I had as hard as I could into his friend and they both fell. People were starting to come over and that must have spooked them, because they ran off. I went over to check on the man still lying on the concrete. His wife was already by his side. He was bloody but conscious and seemed ok. I helped him up. He and his wife thanked me for coming over to help.

"I thought I was a goner," he said.

"I'm just glad you're ok. Scenes like this aren't safe."

I helped him get to his car, then went back to the van. Katie was waiting inside. I hopped in and she drove away.

"That was pretty stupid you know!" she scolded.

"I know, I know, but I wasn't going to just stand there and watch them kill someone."

"Are you ok? Looks like you're bleeding," she said. I looked at my arm.

"I might have torn some stitches." I unwrapped the bandage. Sure enough. The struggle had ripped some stitches out.

"Do you need to go to the hospital?"

"I don't think so, it's just a few. Maybe I can wrap it up good and tight. I have some extra bandage from the hospital. Let's drive a little farther and see what else is out here."

"Ok, but let's not get out of the van again. I can get footage through the window."

I nodded in agreement.

We drove past some more large stores that were getting looted and parked towards the back of the lot to get some footage while I did an off-the-cuff narrative of the scene. We did see some police and guardsmen at some of the stores.

Good, they're trying to get a handle on it.

We took some shots of the streets. There were places where the electricity was out. Some officers on the streets were trying to dissuade the looters, but there just weren't enough of them. We decided we had enough footage and headed back to the station. We took the camera into my office and downloaded the footage. I sent it to the boss so he could decide what to use. Katie went back to her office.

My bandage was getting pretty soaked with blood, so I went to the break room to see if there was a first aid kit. There was one in the cabinet and I took it into the bathroom to try to clean up my arm. Bandages, but not a lot of gauze. I put some adhesive strips over the stitches that were bleeding and then tried to wrap the rest with the little bit of gauze. *I'll have to fix it when I get home.*

I went back to the break room. It had been a long time since breakfast. I pulled out the two protein bars and got some water. Someone had made coffee, so I took a cup of it too. The coffee made me think of Elle again.

"Not nearly as good as yours," I said out loud.

"What's not as good?" Katie asked, walking up next to me to grab a cup.

I was a little startled. "Oh, I didn't know you were there."

"So . . . what's not as good?" she asked again with a little smile and sat down next to me.

"The coffee. My friend owned a shop not far from here." I took a sip and made a face.

"Coffee Expressions?" Katie sipped hers and made the same face as she grabbed some sugar packets.

I looked at her, "Yeah, that's it."

"I've been there several times. She does have good coffee," she smiled.

I just nodded my head, looking down at the table.

"Is she missing?" asked Katie quietly.

I nodded my head again but couldn't meet her gaze.

She laid her hand on my arm, "I'm really sorry, John."

I cleared my throat. "Thanks."

Changing the subject, I asked if the boss had looked at the footage yet.

"Come with me," she said, standing up. We went into Charlie's office, coffee in hand. He just looked at me, then turned his screen toward us and came around the desk. He was watching the footage of the looting. As we watched, I saw again the young couple attacked, but the footage didn't stop there. Katie had kept the camera rolling when I ran in to help. I watched myself grab the first guy and throw him down, and then get attacked by the second guy. Watching it made me realize how really stupid that was.

"What were you thinking?" demanded Charlie.

"Sorry . . . I know it was really stupid and dangerous, but I couldn't just stand there." I looked him in the eye apologetically.

He looked at me thoughtfully. "I'm going to put it on the air because it turned out ok. Could just have easily gone the other way though," he said sternly.

I nodded in agreement. "Right. But you can use it?"

"Yes," he sighed. "A Good Samaritan story is what we all need right now. Why don't you two go home for the night. I'll see you back here in the morning."

Katie and I walked out of the office. "You were supposed to get in the van, not keep recording!" I scolded.

She sassed back, "You were the crazy one running off like a knight in shining armor! Besides, I had one hand on the van door, just in case. See you tomorrow," she said as she opened her car door.

"Yeah, see you tomorrow." And we both drove away.

I headed back home. I desperately needed a shower and clean clothes. When I got to my apartment there was no electricity.

"G r e a t," I said to myself. A cold shower was not what I had anticipated. I went in and checked the fridge. Looked like it had been off for quite a while; nothing was cold. I ran the hot water, hoping it would at least still be warm. No such luck, all cold. I checked my mailbox out of habit. Of course, there was no mail. The apartment building looked pretty abandoned—I hoped only because of the power outage.

Elle's shop had electricity.

I decided to pack a suitcase and head back over there. I took everything I thought I'd need, including any food that still looked good and got back in my car. The events of the last two days just kept running through my head. I got back to Elle's, parked in the back, and carried all my stuff in.

Every time I walked into that shop, I could see Elle's smiling face, and that emptied me of all my strength. I tried to shut my brain off and carried my stuff upstairs. Muffin was there to greet me. I put my stuff down and picked her up. This time she just laid in my arms and purred. I sat her down and gave her more food and water. I took my bag into the bedroom. This was the first time I had really looked around in here. She had a picture of her and her mom on her dresser. I picked it up and touched her face, then let out a groan and told myself to *Stop It!* I put the picture back down and unpacked some things and decided to get in the shower. The water was good and hot, and I just stood in it. My emotions were boiling to the surface and I couldn't control them any longer. I stopped fighting it and let the tears come. All my heart aches, all my fears, poured out into the hot water. I don't know how long I was in there. It seemed like the tears would never end. I was so emotionally drained I couldn't think. I turned off the water, got out and put on some sweats. My stitches needed some attention, so I found the gauze the hospital had given me. I examined them a little more closely. The torn ones didn't look great but I tried closing them with some fresh adhesive strips and then wrapped them all up in the gauze bandage. I stretched out on the couch. Somehow it didn't feel right to lay in Elle's bed. Exhaustion took hold and I drifted off to sleep.

CHAPTER 6

The Crash

M UFFIN woke me up again, but this time didn't scare me. I
stayed there petting her while she purred. There was something comforting about a cat's purr. I checked the time, no need to
rush. Coffee sounded so good. I made my way down to the shop
to see if I could make another pot. *I'm getting pretty good at this!*

My mind went back to Danny as I drank my coffee.

"God" I said out loud, "if you're real—help me to see it." Why
didn't I get his phone number when I was there! *You blew that one,
John.* I had cereal for breakfast and got ready for work. It only took
a few minutes to get there because the coffee shop was so close.

As I got out of the car, Katie pulled up. She asked me how my
night was. I wasn't going to tell her I completely fell apart . . . .so I
said, "Good. How about you?" She shrugged in response.

When we got in the office, everyone was watching the World
News screen. The stock market was crashing, I mean 1929 crashing. It had been dropping significantly everyday, but this was bad.
If you had money invested, it was gone, along with people's retirement. Everyone knew we were in trouble. This would cascade into
jobs lost, government food lines . . . 'The Grapes of Wrath' ran
through my mind. Analysts talked about a world bank system as a
possible solution. I could see the look of panic in everyone's eyes.

My boss called a meeting, so we all went into the break room.

"I haven't heard anything from the owner/producer yet. Until I do, we will continue to do our jobs. And our job is to report facts! We do not need to spread unsubstantiated rumors. Keep that in mind." He motioned for everyone to get back to work, then added, "John and Katie, can you come in my office?" We followed him in.

"I'll send you back out on the streets this morning. See if you can *safely* (looking at me) get some reactions to the crash."

"Yes sir," we said and walked out.

"I'll go get the camera equipment," I offered.

She nodded, "I'll be there in a minute." We met at the van. "Where to this time?" she asked.

"Hmmm . . . " I didn't have any good ideas. "Let's just get out there and see what we find."

I hopped in the passenger side. We drove in silence for a while, and then Katie pulled over.

"John. What do you think is going to happen?"

Our eyes locked for a second, then we both looked away, neither one of us wanting to show the growing fear inside.

"Katie, do you believe in God?" I asked, staring straight ahead.

"I guess so," she said hesitantly.

"Do you think the rapture happened?" I asked, looking for her eyes.

She met my gaze. "Is that what you think happened?"

I sighed. "Maybe, I've never really thought too much about God, but my friend was a believer."

"Your friend . . . from the coffee shop?" she clarified.

"Yes. Elle. And she's gone. Her brother was not a believer and he's still here. He thinks it was the rapture."

Katie looked away. "Remember when I said my sister in Wisconsin hadn't been heard from? She was a believer. She used to try to talk to me about Jesus, but I always changed the subject. I haven't heard from her husband or two kids either. I think they are all gone."

"Maybe that's the story we should be following." I threw it out there. "Let's interview some people that lost someone, see if they were Christians."

She slowly nodded her head in agreement. I felt like we had a plan and that made me a little hopeful.

"Why don't we go by a few churches—see if anyone is there," I said.

"Ok, which way?"

I pulled out my phone and tapped in 'churches near me'. There were several, so I started directions to the closest. It was only six minutes from where we were. We parked in the lot and tried all the doors. They were all locked and it didn't seem like anyone was there. There was a man across the street watching us from his porch, so we walked over.

"Did you go to this church?" I asked, as I showed him my ID. "We're doing a story on church members".

"No."

"Have you seen any members back here since the disappearances?"

"No," he said again and went back in his house, locking the door with a loud click. Katie and I looked at each other.

"I guess he had nothing to say," she said with a shrug.

We walked back to the van and got in. I put directions in for the next church. As we drove, we came upon a large supermarket that was still being looted. Katie stopped on the side of the street.

"What?" I searched the scene, thinking she saw something.

"Are you worried you will run out of food?" she asked.

I looked at her and then the store. "Are you out of groceries?"

"Nearly. I was getting pretty low when all this happened. Nothing has opened up to go buy food. Maybe this is my only option." She was serious . . .

"You're going to loot?" I said softly.

"I don't want to, but I'm scared. What if the stores never open back up?"

It was a possibility that we tried not to think about.

She looked me in the eye. "Come with me. We'll leave the van down the street so it doesn't look like the station is involved."

"There are probably cameras all over the place," I said, looking all around us.

"Please. I don't want to go in alone!" she begged.

This didn't feel right, but I agreed. Someone had left a ball cap in the van. I grabbed it and pulled it low over my eyes. She pulled her hood up and threw on some sunglasses.

We got out and started walking across the parking lot towards the store. I grabbed a cart someone had left, then remembered the last time I was in a store parking lot and looked around again. Everyone seemed focused on their own task. I was hopeful it would stay that way. The scene in the store was unbelievable. Instead of the neat, full shelves we were used to, it looked like a war zone. Unwanted items covered the floor, entire shelves bare. It was difficult to push the cart through the mess. We walked quickly through the aisles looking for anything edible. There were some canned items left and we found some pasta items. The meat and bakery sections were empty. The liquor shelves were cleaned out. No toilet paper, paper towels, or napkins. There were some bags of cat food left so I grabbed a few of those. We had maybe half a cart of items when I started feeling paranoid.

"Let's get out of here." I pulled my hat even lower as we left, hoping no one would recognize me. About halfway across the lot there was man watching us. I steered the cart away from him and tried to look as big as I could.

It works for bears.

We got to the van, unloaded as fast as we could, and got out of there. I felt pretty guilty about it, and promised myself when that store opened back up, I would pay them.

Katie pulled over a few blocks down. She was visibly shaken.

"Want me to drive?" I offered. She got out, so I slid over and waited for her to get in the passenger side.

"I'm so sorry . . . " she said. I could tell she was fighting tears.

"Hey, it's ok," I assured her.

She put her hands over her face in shame. "I didn't mean to turn you into a thief."

"We'll make it right when the store opens back up," I said, trying to smile.

"Do you think it will? Open back up?" She was studying my eyes.

"I don't know," I answered honestly, and we both looked away.

I drove on to the next church. It also looked empty, but when we tried the door, it was open. I stepped in and hollered, "Hello! Anyone here?" It was dark in the hall. I found a light switch, but it didn't work. "The power must be out." We walked down the dark hall till we came to an open foyer. It was lighter here as there were several windows.

"Hello?" I hollered again. There was a door marked 'office' that was slightly open, so we went over to it. "Wait out here a minute," I told Katie, as I started inside. The office was very dark. I found another light switch and tried it . . . nothing. I got out my phone and turned on the flashlight. It looked like this was a reception area. There were chairs and a desk. Behind the desk were some cabinets with a coffee pot and supplies on the counter. I started to go towards another door when someone ran into me. We both fell to the floor. I threw myself on him, pinning him down. Katie came running in with her phone light on.

He gasped, "I don't have any money!"

"Look buddy, I'm not trying to rob you. We're reporters. We just want to ask you a few questions. I'm going to get off, ok?"

He stopped struggling, so I got off and offered him my hand to help him up. After a second, he took it, still looking at us a little suspiciously. He was a young guy, maybe early twenties.

"Did you go to church here?" I asked.

"No. Well, I came a couple of times. My college roommate used to come here. He invited me a few times, that's why I was hanging out. I thought maybe he'd show up."

"So, you haven't seen him since Monday, when people went missing?"

He shook his head. "He worked with the youth. I thought maybe he was here."

"Have you seen anyone?" Katie asked.

"No," he answered nervously. "They're all gone. Can I go now?"

"Of course, sorry for the scare!" I answered. He left quickly.

We walked back to the van. I was feeling pretty discouraged.

"Maybe we need a different approach," I said, as we got back in.

"Should we ask about the stock market crash? It's what the boss is expecting," Katie suggested. She was right, he would be expecting something about the crash.

"Let's go over to the business district," I said, as I started the engine. We drove in silence until I pulled up in front of the 'high end' offices. Katie grabbed her camera and panned up and down the block.

"Let's just go in, see who's here," I said. There was a receptionist in the main lobby. She was wiping her eyes and put her tissue away when she saw us approaching. I quickly read the names on the plaque on the wall.

"Is Dillon Johnson in?" I gave her my ID and explained we were doing a story on the market crash.

"Do you have an appointment?" she asked.

"No, but we'd like to ask him a few questions."

"I'm sorry, but Mr. Johnson isn't available without an appointment." She sounded like she had said this multiple times today.

"Is there anyone else we could speak with?"

"I'll check. You can wait over there," and she nodded towards some chairs along the wall.

We walked to the chairs and sat down. It seemed like there were a lot of people leaving with boxes in their hands, like they were cleaning out their offices. I stood up and walked over to one guy just coming off the elevator, showed him my ID and asked him, "Can you tell me what's happening here?"

"We've all been let go, that's what's happening!" he said rather loudly. He was obviously not happy about it.

"Everyone? Can you tell me why?" I was puzzled.

He snapped back, "The money is gone. All of it! Everything I invested!"

Just then there was a loud crash outside and a car alarm went off. The guy I was talking to ran to the front door, and I was just behind him. He ran up to the car that was sounding the alarm and pushed some people out of the way. The scene looked like a Hollywood horror set. Someone had jumped out of a window and landed on a car. The guy I was talking to let out a gut-wrenching scream and ran off. Katie came up behind me. When she saw what had happened, she gasped with a look of terror on her face. I wrapped my arm around her shoulder and walked her away from the scene. When we got to the van, I put my arms around her. She was silently sobbing as I held her.

"I don't know if I can take all this!" she cried, trying to compose herself.

She took a tissue out of her purse. I opened the van door and helped her in. I wished I had some words of comfort for her. I wanted to tell her everything would be alright, but I was pretty sure it would get worse before it got better.

I drove back to the station. We both needed a break. I parked next to her car so we could discreetly move the groceries into her trunk.

"Why don't you take something," she offered.

"No, really, I'm good for now. I just need the cat food."

She handed me a jar of peach jam anyway, and I took it. I told her to just head home, I would report to the boss. She gave me a hug and then left. I went in and explained what had happened. Charlie seemed a little distracted, just told me to write it up and email it to him. I went into my office, sent him the email with the camera footage, and headed home.

Home . . . really, it was Elle's home. When I opened the apartment door, Muffin came running over. I picked her up. There was that beautiful purr again. I sat down with her. She started kneading my arm. I never really cared for cats before—before . . . so much had changed in three days.

CHAPTER 7

The Invitation

I N the morning I took inventory on my food supply. I figured in about two weeks I'd be out of everything. I might have a few things left in my apartment I could bring over. I'll have to check later today. The president was on TV last night trying to squelch the panic. He promised the trucks would be rolling soon with supplies for every city. I was pretty skeptical. The World News was reporting that factories and production centers had folded and nothing was being shipped right now. Businesses had to be approved as "essential" to operate. I wondered what happened to the volunteers that usually helped after a disaster. Were they gone too?

I made sure Muffin had plenty to eat and fresh water before I left for work. When I got there, everyone was gathered in the break room. I saw Katie and walked over to her.

"What's going on?" I looked around the room at all the weary, strained faces.

She grabbed my arm and held on. "The boss has an announcement; I'm afraid it's not going to be good."

Oh boy, this is where we all get fired.

Charlie walked into the room looking tired and unshaven. As always, he got right to the point.

"The producers have notified me that we will not be doing any more live newscasts. The National News will be broadcasting from this station for the foreseeable future. Thank you all for your hard work and dedication. Please take care of yourselves." And he walked out.

Following a moment of stunned silence, people trickled out of the room, talking quietly to each other.

I looked at Katie. "I'm not surprised."

"Me neither, but I had hoped for a little more time." She swallowed hard and let go of my arm.

"What are your plans?" I asked her as we walked back to her office.

"I—I don't know, how about you?" She seemed to be struggling to keep moving.

Now I took her arm to guide her. "Let's go in your office for a minute."

We went in and I closed the door. Turning toward Katie, I told her that I had researched some doomsday preppers a while back and saw something interesting. "It seems there was a group of Christians that were gathering supplies to give to the needy in a doomsday scenario. I'm going to see if I can find them, or at least their underground bunkers." She looked at me like I was a little crazy, and I had to admit, it sounded crazy when I said it out loud.

"John, please be careful! Those doomsday preppers are heavily armed."

"I will, for sure!" Now I felt a little embarrassed that I had shared that with her. I guess I thought she would want to help me.

"Ok, well, take care of yourself!" I said and gave her an awkward hug. Then I went to my office to clean out any personal items. I threw a few items in a box and looked around.

So this is it . . .

Not exactly how I envisioned my first real reporting job ending. I said a few goodbyes to some of the other employees and then left.

"What am I going to do now," I muttered under my breath as I drove away. I went back to the coffee shop. It was the only place that felt 'right'.

I spent the next week watching the news go from bad to worse. Gas shortages, food shortages, internet was spotty, cell towers randomly went down, electricity was in and out. There were no real leads on the 'preppers', so I wrote that idea off. I had long conversations with Muffin, who was always ready to listen. I was pretty sure I was losing my mind.

"I've got to get out!" I told Muffin. She rubbed my leg. Gas was a problem. There was about half a tank left in my car. Maybe one of the nearby gas stations had gotten a shipment in. I could take a short drive to see. I wondered where Danny was. How stupid of me to not get his phone number or address where he was staying! Could he still be at that little church?

I decided to drive that way in search of gas. Station after station was closed. I got to the little church and parked. I went to the door and knocked. No one answered. I tried to see in the window, but it looked dark inside. Could be the electricity was out. I went back to the car and rummaged through the glove box looking for some paper. There was an old envelope that would work. I wrote:

> Danny,
> I'm trying to contact you. My number is 555-3456.
> I'm staying at the coffee shop.
> John

I pushed the note under the door, then drove back to my apartment and grabbed more clothes, a flashlight, batteries, and any food left in the kitchen. I also threw in more towels and blankets, then got back in the car, taking a slightly different route, still looking for an open station. Nothing. I got back to the coffee shop thinking that was a waste of gas.

The coffee shop still looked like it had been ransacked, so I started cleaning up. I swept, wiped off tables and countertops, and tried to put things away. The cash register was still hanging open, so I closed it. It looked like the place I remembered again . . . minus Elle. I went back up to the apartment and sat on the couch. Reality crashed over me like an ocean wave in rough waters. What was I going to do? My food was nearly gone, travel was out for lack of gas . . . where would I go, anyway? A sense of despair swept over me like I had never known.

"Dear Lord," I prayed. "I need you." I had never given myself over to God. I had too many doubts and insecurities to let myself believe. But I was stripped bare, exposed, and I finally let go. "I believe in you Jesus, and I need your help!" Emotions were pouring out of me, but somewhere in the mess that was me, I could feel His presence. A peace I had never known, that gave me hope again. I was raw and cut open, and He gave me peace.

I went to sleep that night more peaceful than I had been in years. My dreams were good. Elle and I were making coffee together, laughing and talking.

I couldn't breathe . . . all of a sudden, I couldn't breathe! As I came out of that dream, I realized there was a knee on my chest and started to struggle. Now I was fully awake, looking at a gun jammed into my forehead. I stopped moving.

"Now you got it!" snarled a man in his late 20's. "Just hold nice and still." He took his knee off my chest but kept the gun on my forehead. With his free hand he threw a zip tie at me.

"Put this around your wrists," and he smiled at me, not in a nice way. My heart was about to jump out of my chest and my hands were shaking as I put them through the zip tie.

"Pull it tight with your teeth," he instructed. I did. There is nothing to describe how it feels to tie yourself up. He grabbed my wrists and pulled me off the couch. I crashed into the coffee table again. I started to get up, but he kicked me back down on the floor.

"You get up when I tell you to!" he screamed.

"Look, I don't have anyth . . . " I started to say when his boot hit my stomach. I couldn't breathe, again.

"Don't talk!" he ordered.

As I lay gasping for air he started walking around the apartment. I could tell he was high on something.

Lord, is this going to be it for me?

He was going through all the cabinets, either looking for food or drugs. He wasn't going to find either.

Muffin peaked out from behind a cabinet and he went after her.

"Hey!" I yelled. "It's just a cat, she won't hurt you!"

That infuriated him. He grabbed my shirt and threw me into the wall, then punched me in the jaw. I could feel the blood pouring into my mouth.

"I said No Talking!" he screamed in my face. Then he went back into the kitchen and started throwing everything out of the cabinets. I was spitting out blood, desperately trying to think of a way to escape. I had seen some videos of people breaking out of zip ties and wondered if it really worked.

How did he get in here without me hearing him? I must have forgotten to lock the doors.

I just sat on the floor spitting blood . . . waiting . . . for a chance to run, or for him to use his gun.

When he realized there was nothing in any of the cabinets, he came over to me again, put his gun to my head and said, "You must have something here I could use. Where are you hiding it?" I hesitated to talk. He jammed the gun under my chin and screamed, "Where Is It?!"

"I don't have anything!" I shouted back, and closed my eyes, waiting for the blow, when the door flew open, and someone jumped on the guy. The gun went flying across the room as the two bodies crashed to the floor. It took me a second to realize what was happening. It was Danny! He was wrestling with this guy on the floor. I got up and tried to snap the zip tie the way I had seen. It worked! My hands were free. He had gotten Danny on the floor and was punching him. I wrapped my arms around him, trying to stop the punches and pull him off. I couldn't hold him so I pushed him and dove for the gun, but he was on top of me. We wrestled on the floor again, punching and kicking. How was this guy so strong? He pushed me away and made a lunge for the gun, but Danny had gotten there first. The guy was insane. He lunged at Danny, knocking the gun down and started punching him again. I grabbed the gun and hit him on the head, hard. He went limp.

I stood there in disbelief, trying to catch my breath. Danny and I looked at each other.

"You came in the nick of time," I panted. "How did you know I needed you?"

"I got your note at the church and I came to make sure you were alright. The door to the coffee shop was hanging open when I got here. I didn't think that looked right, so I came in quietly. Then I heard shouting coming from up here, so I crept up the stairs. I cracked the door and saw him standing over you. I had to do something, so I jumped on him!"

"I'm glad you did, you saved my life!" and I gave him my hand, helping him off the floor. "We better tie this guy up in case he comes to." I grabbed a light cord and tied his hands and feet.

"How did he get in here?" asked Danny.

I blinked, then shook my head. "I guess I forgot to lock the doors last night. I know—stupid mistake!"

"John, I was coming to ask if you wanted to come with us. We are going to Janet and Bill's farm in southern Missouri. They have 40 acres with a large garden. They've been canning all summer so plenty of food, with chickens and some cows. It's not safe here for you."

I almost cried . . . "Yes! Yes, I will gladly come."

Danny smiled at my enthusiasm. "Great! Pack up whatever you need. Do you have any gas?"

"Half a tank in the car," I answered.

"We have a large van to get us there. Could we siphon out your gas to take with us?"

"Of course!"

Danny went down to get a gas can while I packed. I filled my duffel bag that I had brought over and then pulled one of Elle's suitcases from under the bed. I packed anything I thought we could use, towels, blankets, meds, personal items, even utensils. Muffin finally came out of hiding and rubbed my leg. "Want to go on a little road trip?" I got the cat crate I had seen in the closet and put her in it, with her supplies in a separate bag. I did a last walk through of the apartment. Then I saw the picture of Elle and her mom on her nightstand. I tucked that in my satchel as well. Phones were down, so I couldn't call the police to pick up the guy on my floor. The police station wasn't far. We could stop on the way out of town. And there was one more stop I wanted to make on the way. Katie's place.

CHAPTER 8

The Stories

I MET Danny down in the coffee shop. He had finished siphoning the gas from my car. We put everything in his Ford Fiesta and headed to the police station.

"Danny, would it be ok if we also stopped by my friend Katie's house? I want to make sure she is alright."

"Sure, I just need the directions."

When we finished filing a report at the police station, I gave him the address.

"I'll just be a minute," I said as I got out of the car. I walked up to the small duplex and knocked. At first it seemed no one was there, but then I saw her peeking out of the blinds that covered the front window. I waved my hand at her and she answered the door. "John! You scared me a little."

"Sorry! I just wanted to be sure you were ok. How's the food holding up?"

"I'm trying to ration it until some stores open back up. I don't think it's going to last though."

She looked tired and thinner than I remembered.

"Do you have anyplace else to go?" I asked, looking back at Danny. He smiled and nodded his head at me. "Because some friends invited me to go with them down south to a farm. There's plenty of food and livestock there. If you have no place to go, you are welcome to come with us."

She looked at me the way I looked at Danny when he invited me. With a little gasp she said, "Are you sure it will be ok?"

Danny was getting out of the car now and walked up. "Pack up whatever you'll need," and smiled at her.

She gave us both a hug and ran back inside to throw some things in a suitcase.

"You wouldn't have any gasoline in a car or in a can?" Danny asked her.

"No gas cans, there's a little left in my car."

"Could I try to siphon it out? We have a large van to get everyone to the farm, but could use some spare gas."

"Sure!" she said.

I waited for her in the living room while she packed. Danny went out to get the gas.

"You are a real Godsend!" and she handed me one of her bags.

I smiled. There was a lot of that happening today, starting with Danny saving my life. I'd have to tell her the story sometime. I helped her out to the car with her bags. The Fiesta was getting pretty cramped, but we didn't have far to go to get to the van. I got to see the 'merry band of misfits' (as I dubbed them in my head) for the first time. It looked like that same small group of people that were in the church plus Katie and me. We shook hands and Danny introduced everyone. We packed everything in the van and piled in. There was seating for 10 so we had plenty of room. I learned the farm belonged to Bill Garcia and his wife Janet. They had been in Saint Louis on a weekend getaway when people disappeared. Somehow, everyone had wound up in that little church. Another God thing I imagined.

We drove in silence for a little while, then Danny said, "Funny how we all ended up here, like it was meant to be!" Everyone chuckled a little, but I could tell we were all playing those memories back in our heads, at least I was. Then Katie asked Luke how he wound up here, in the van.

Luke smiled a little at her, then looked at Danny.

"That's a good question, I'll have to go back to the beginning to answer it."

Then Luke told his story: "My parents fought a lot, and they split up when I was in junior high. My dad moved away, so I stayed with my mom. When I was in high school her latest boyfriend, Gus, moved in. He didn't like me, and the feeling was mutual. At first it was ok, I stayed out of the house when I knew he would be there. Then he got laid off at the factory and was there all the time. One morning before I left for school, he pinned me up against the wall, mad about something I hadn't put away.

When I got to school Danny could see something was wrong, so I told him the story. He was my best friend since grade school. We joked about 'taking Gus down' if he tried that again! When I got home that night I went straight to my room, but when I went to the kitchen to grab something to eat, he was in there. I didn't say anything to him, just opened the fridge, and he grabbed my arm, yanking me around. He was hollering about how expensive food was and that I better get a job if I was going to eat so much. I yelled "maybe YOU need to get a job!" and he slapped me across the face so hard I fell backwards on the stove. My mom came running in and screamed at me to get to my room. I wanted to fight him, but knew he would probably kill me, so I went to my room. I could hear them talking in the kitchen, then mom came into my room. She hollered at me! Like it was my fault! She said something about me trying to sabotage her relationship with Gus and stormed out.

The next morning, I left early for school so I wouldn't have to see either of them. I hadn't eaten anything since school lunch the day before. At lunch I met up with Danny, telling him what had happened. He told me to come home with him; I could eat dinner with him and Elle.

It was after nine when I went back home, hoping I could just sneak in, but they were both in the kitchen, waiting for me. That's when they told me they were going to move to Indiana, that Gus was going to try to get work there. Then Gus said, "You better just stay here." I looked at my mom, but she wouldn't meet my gaze.

"Where, exactly, am I supposed to stay? I'm a junior in high school!"

Then he started yelling about me quitting school and getting a job, about being a man, and my mom just stood there! I ran out of the house. I had no place to go, so I spent the night at the high school, sleeping in the doorway.

At lunch I grabbed some food and took it to the baseball field and sat on the bleachers. Danny came looking for me and sat down on the bleachers next to me. I told him the whole story and he said, "You could stay with us." He said he had talked to Elle about what was happening, and she suggested it. At first, I said no because I knew they had financial issues after their mom died. But Danny wouldn't take no for an answer. That night Danny came home with me and helped me pack. As we were leaving, I looked at my mom . . . she just turned and walked away." Luke stopped talking, obviously shaken by the memory.

Everyone was quiet for a few minutes. Then Katie asked, "How did you wind up at the church?"

Danny picked it up from there: "Luke and I got part time jobs and helped with the bills. Elle was trying to work her way through college. After we graduated, we got a small apartment and took full time jobs at the Radio Barn, the one that was by the church. That morning we were talking in the parking lot, waiting for the manager to get there and open up, when his car pulled into the lot and crashed into the light pole! We both ran over, but there was no one in the car! Then cars started crashing into each other on the streets. It was unreal! We went around to several of the crash sites to see if we could help. Some people were injured, but some of the cars were empty. We did what we could for anyone that was hurt. Luke looked at me and said, "What is going on!?" I was afraid I knew, I just kept saying "No . . . No . . . God No!" That's when I noticed the church and ran over there. Luke followed me; he thought I had lost it. It was open so we went in. I sat in a pew and picked up a Bible."

Now Luke was talking: "I really did think he had lost it. He just sat there staring at that Bible. I knew his sister was a Christian, but Danny never put any faith in that stuff. I finally took the Bible out of his hand and said, "What are you thinking?" The way he looked at me, he scared me, like he had just realized some horror. He took the Bible back and opened it to Revelation and started telling me about the prophecy of the church being raptured. He tried to call Elle, but she didn't answer. That's when Megan came in. She started telling us how . . . ." He paused a minute.

"Megan, why don't you tell the rest?" She looked at Luke a little hesitant. "Just start at the beginning, like you told us in the church."

And we listened as Megan picked up the story: "My dad was a Major in the Air Force, so we moved around a lot. I would just get settled in a school and start to make friends and we would have to move again. About two years ago we moved to Valparaiso, Florida when my dad was transferred to Elgin Air Force Base. It was my freshman year, so all the kids were new to the school, which made it easier to fit in. Heather sat next to me in music class, and we had English together. We became good friends and I would spend the night at her house often. I loved going there because she had horses and we would ride together. There's something so freeing when you're galloping on a horse; it's like you're flying, without a care in the world! I finally felt like I fit in somewhere. I would go there and help clean stalls and keep the horses brushed. I even helped bale hay.

Then six months ago, my dad was transferred to Scott Air Force Base and he said we were moving to Saint Louis. I ran up to my room and cried all night. He and my mom both tried to talk to me, but I wouldn't listen. I screamed at them, 'I hate you!' Of course, we moved anyway and I shut them out of my life. I purposely made friends with the kids I knew my mom would not approve of. Our neighbors started inviting us to go to church with them and mom and dad went, but I refused. I was surprised when they kept going; they never showed any interest in church before. I could see something changing in them, but I was still so bitter about Dad's job and having to move all the time that I wouldn't listen to them.

There was a senior boy, Jacob, that kept asking me out but my parents wouldn't let me go. I snuck out one night and met him at the corner. He had a car and we drove around for a while. He also had a fake ID and tried to buy some beer at the gas station, but they wouldn't sell it to him. When he took me home, my dad was waiting at the door. We had a big shouting match and I was grounded for two weeks. That's when I decided I was going to run away. I set it up with Jacob. He was going to go with me. We were going to meet at school and just drive away, maybe into Illinois where no one knew us. It was Monday morning and we met in the parking lot. I had thrown some clothes and personal things in my backpack. As we drove away, I was feeling pretty guilty . . . I had left an awful note on my bed. That's when all the cars started crashing into each other. Jacob tried to avoid them, but there was a chain reaction—everyone was crashing into someone. We were hit and spun around and then an SUV broadsided us on Jacob's side. When we all stopped moving, I looked at him and he was unconscious and bleeding. The door wouldn't open so I crawled out the window and started screaming for help! A few men came over and tried to get him out of the car, but the doors wouldn't open! One of them checked for a pulse through the broken window and shook his head. I couldn't believe it! This wasn't real! I ran until I couldn't run any more, then I fell to the ground, sobbing." Megan closed her eyes, then opened them and took a deep breath. "I needed to get home to my mom, so I got up and started running again. The school was maybe two miles from my house. As I ran, I saw people on the streets screaming for someone. There were accidents everywhere. The sound of sirens rang in the air. Breathlessly, I ran into the house, hollering for Mom and Dad. They should've been there; Dad was working from home that day. I checked the driveway and both cars were still there. I ran to my room and flung myself on the bed, still sobbing. I laid there for a long time. I didn't know what to do or who to call. When I got out of the bed, I noticed the note was on my floor. I really hoped my parents hadn't seen it.

I went down to the kitchen and saw Mom's Bible open on the table. It was open to John chapter three, and she had underlined something. I read, 'For God so loved the world, that He gave His one and only Son, that whoever believes in Him shall not perish, but have eternal life.' I picked up the Bible and went to the neighbors that had invited them to church, but no one was there either. I needed to go to that church. It wasn't far, only a few blocks.

When I stepped inside, Danny and Luke were there. I started to leave, but Danny smiled and asked me to stay. He asked if I went to this church and I started to cry, and told him about my parents, how they tried to get me to come. And I told him about me running away, and the car accident. He and Luke just sat with me, listening, as I poured out my heart.

I was going through my mom's Bible, looking at all the verses she had underlined, reading them out loud, and came across Romans 10 verse 9: 'If you confess with your mouth, Jesus is Lord, and believe in your heart that God raised him from the dead, you will be saved.' Right then and there, Danny, Luke and I said that we believed, and asked Jesus to be our Lord and Savior."

Luke reached over and squeezed Megan's hand saying, "Shortly after that, Bill and Janet came in."

Janet turned to look at us from the front seat and shared their story:

"Bill and I were excited about celebrating our 25th wedding anniversary. We planned – well, I did most of the planning – to go to St. Louis and visit the big city. We don't get away from the family farm very often. Bill grew up there and I love the farm life, but we just wanted a get-away. My nephew, Jamie, has lived with us since he was 12 and he is almost as tall as Bill now. He loves the farm too, and we hope he will carry on with it.

We drove the big van up. Bill had scheduled some body work with a shop in Saint Louis that had some original parts. Of course, on the way up we started to have engine trouble so also had to have that looked at. Fortunately, the same shop could do both, so we dropped our luggage of at the hotel and then took the van to the shop. We used the city busses to get over to the Arch and walked around on the landing. The car shop called and said he thought it was the starter and he would have it ready the next afternoon. We had a romantic lunch at the Spaghetti Factory.

He was excited about the Cardinals; they had gotten in the playoffs with a wild card game and we went to Ball Park City to watch the game on the big screen. We had stadium food and enjoyed the atmosphere of the game. The excitement of the crowd was catching and we found ourselves on our feet, cheering as the Cards ran the bases. It was a lot more noise than we are used to in the country though, so it was nice to get back to our quiet room and soft bed.

The next morning, we went down to our free breakfast and I pulled out my phone to look at some websites I had researched. The Botanical Gardens opened at 9:00 am and we were going to catch a bus there. Then I suggested going to the Fox Theater that night to see Fiddler on the Roof.

We went down to catch the bus at about 8:00 am. As we drove from stop to stop, I was people-watching. A young man boarded, dressed like he was on his way to work. At the next stop a young mother boarded with two small girls dressed in little princess dresses. She sat across from us and smiled. I told her girls they were both beautiful princesses. The youngest of the two asked me if I knew which princess she was. Shaking my head and leaning over to her I said, 'No, I don't!'

'Elsa!' she told me proudly. Her mom laughed and told me that was her favorite.

We made a few more stops and an elderly couple boarded. The bus driver was very patient as he helped them on the bus and into their seats. They must have been regular riders because he called them by name. As we drove on, I pulled out my phone to look up a few more web sites when I heard a sound or saw a movement. I looked up from my phone and the young mother and her children were gone! Her bags were still there, but they were gone! Then the young man on the bus screamed that the bus driver was gone! Bill and I both looked and the bus was driving with no driver! Bill and this young man both bolted towards the steering wheel. Bill was closer and got there first. He swerved sharply to miss the oncoming traffic, throwing me out of my seat. We clipped a parked car, but he was able to apply the brakes before we hit anything else. We were stopped, blocking both lanes of traffic. He could see another car coming towards us and yelled "hang on!" The oncoming car ran straight into us, jolting the bus. The elderly woman on the bus started screaming, 'George! George!' The young man went back to her to try to help, and she was crying that George was gone! Bill and I just looked at each other. How could people be disappearing! The young man helped her off the bus and we followed. We just stood there for a few minutes, not knowing what to do. Then people started coming out of houses, running down streets, all yelling, looking for someone. The sound of sirens filled the air. Neighbors were attending to the elderly woman, and the young man ran off towards home, I supposed.

Bill and I didn't know where we were, but started walking back the way we thought the hotel was. I pulled out my phone to see if I could get the directions, but the app was not working. Then the phone showed 'no service'. We walked several blocks and more and more people seemed to be on the streets. Car accidents were everywhere, blocking traffic, and we saw several people sitting on the side of the road that were injured. We both went to them to see if we could help, but there wasn't much we could do. We were near a small strip mall and the crowds were getting violent, throwing bricks and rocks into glass windows and doors, breaking in. I was panicking, crying to Bill that we were going to die! That's when he saw the church, and lead me to it, trying to get me to calm down. When we went in, I was still crying and Bill explained how the crowds were breaking into the stores."

Danny added, "Luke and I went outside to see, that's when you got hit, John! We saw you fall and ran over, each grabbing an arm, and dragged you back to the church. Bill came out and helped us carry you in."

I rubbed my head a little, "I remember that part!" Then added "Thanks, by the way . . . "

Janet continued: "After they pulled John in, Megan started softly reading Bible verses. Danny was trying to wake John up, and Bill checked his vitals. Bill said he thought he was ok and would wake up soon. We sat down in the pew and asked if anyone knew what was happening. Danny sat down by us and asked if we believed in God. Then he went on to explain how he believed it was the rapture.

John started to wake up as we were talking, and Danny went over to help him. He showed him where the bathrooms were and came and told us he was going to take John to his sister's coffee shop.

When he came back, we could see he was pretty distraught. He sat down by Luke and told him Elle was gone. He was even more sure that it was the rapture.

The streets were all blocked. No cars could get through and it wasn't safe outside, so we all stayed at the church that night. We talked most of the night about what had happened and Bible prophecy. Bill and I went to a Catholic Church once in a while. Mostly just Christmas. But I had never really given any thought to it, to the Bible. I had never read it. By morning everyone was starving, and I was looking through my bag to see if I had packed any snacks. That's when Megan spoke up and said her house was close and we could all go there to eat. She didn't want to go home alone."

Megan smiled at Janet and said, "We went back and forth from the church to my house most of the next week."

Bill spoke up: "Janet and I talked about coming from the farm and how our van was in a shop somewhere. When I told Danny the name of the shop, Luke said he knew where that was. It was about 10 miles from Megan's house and we had her parents cars, but the roads were not clear enough to get through. It was maybe two days later we decided to try to take a car over there to get it. Some of the roads were clear enough to drive on, so Luke and I picked our way through the maze. The gas stations we passed had lines of cars waiting for gas. Some were already out and had big Closed signs up. We checked the gas gauge in the car. It was nearly full.

The shop door was open when we got there, but there was no one inside. The van was in the garage and the hood was open, like the mechanic had been working on it. Luke looked under the hood and said, 'This could be a problem.' I looked at it. The starter was missing. We looked at each other and sighed, then both started searching for another starter in the shop. I found the old one, but Luke kept looking and finally found the new one. I asked him if he knew how to put that on and he said he thought so. As we found the tools we would need, he told me how his dad had been a mechanic and had let him hang out in the shop sometimes and help. I knew a little bit about engines, mostly tractors, and it took us about two hours to get the starter on. We turned the key and high-fived each other when it started. Then I shook my head, and Luke asked what was wrong. I showed him my gas gauge, it was near empty. I had enough to get back to Megan's house, but was not sure how much farther.

I followed Luke in the car and we went back towards the gas stations that had been open a few hours ago, but every one of them had big signs that said "Out of Gas". I pulled up in front of Megan's and parked, then broke the bad news to Janet. That's when Megan invited us all to stay with her. She said she didn't have anyone else. Janet took me aside and we talked for a minute. Then we both went back to the group and she said, 'Why don't you all come home with us to the farm? We have a big house with enough bedrooms for everyone and I canned fruits and vegetables all summer, so the pantry is full!'

We talked about the not so small gas problem. We could all fit in the van easily but would need a full tank and some to spare to make the 4-hour trip back. That's when we hatched the plan to siphon gas from as many cars as we could to fill the tank and any extra gas cans we could find. That took us most of the next week."

Danny looked at me and said, "We were getting ready to leave and I went back to the church one more time. That's when I found your note. We were using Megan's mom's car to pick up some things from our apartment. I talked to Bill and told him I needed to check on you and I asked if there would be room for one more. He said, 'There is *always* room for one more.'

I caught Bill's eyes in the rearview mirror and smiled at him. He smiled back.

Janet looked back at us. "We have a few more hours to drive, is everyone ok?" We all said yes.

"Well, I might need to find a bathroom soon," she laughed.

"Honey, that might be hard with everything closed." Then Bill added, "But I can find a big bush!"

We all laughed.

We had been on the road for over an hour and I hadn't seen one other car. Occasionally, there was an abandoned car on the side of the road. Danny whispered something to Bill and he nodded his head. I looked at Danny inquisitively.

He explained, "I suggested we stop by the next abandoned car and see if we can get some gas out of it."

Bill said, "I have a gas tank on the farm that is pretty full, but who knows when we can get that filled again."

We drove another twenty minutes or so when we saw two cars left on the side of the highway. Bill pulled over just behind them and said, "Wait in here for a minute while I check it out."

Danny and I looked at each other and both got out with him. We scanned the area, quietly walking up to the cars, and looked in the windows. There was no one with either car. Danny walked back to the van. "It's fine. You can get out and stretch your legs if you want." He went around to the back of the van and got the gas can and hose. Everyone got out of the van and walked around.

Bill hollered, "Hey hon! There's a big bush over there!"

"I see it! You all stay here!" she laughed and headed for the bush.

We piled back in the van and drove in silence for a bit. Then Megan asked Katie how she wound up here.

Katie shared her story: "My mom and dad met in Korea. He was in the army, stationed over there. They fell in love, got married, and moved back to the states when he left the army. My mom held on to her Buddhism customs after they moved here, so that was pretty much all I knew growing up. I didn't really hold to any of the teachings though. I wasn't sure any religion was real. My older sister had started attending a Christian church in high school. She had a friend that kept inviting her. My mom wasn't too happy about it. My sister was already gone from the house, and when I went away to college, my parents moved back to Korea. After people disappeared, when John told me he thought it was the rapture of the church, well, at first I didn't believe it. But I couldn't get it out of my mind, you know? Then, after we lost our jobs, I was alone in my apartment with nothing to do but think. I wished I had a Bible so I could read what it said. I tried a Bible app, but my internet was in and out. I started to pray, asking for protection, and help, even though I wasn't sure anyone was listening. Two days later, John and Danny showed up on my doorstep." She looked at me and smiled. Then continued, "After hearing everyone's story, I have no doubt that God is here with us. That he brought us all together for a reason." Everyone in the van agreed. This "motley crew of misfits" really was a miracle from God.

Danny looked at me, "John, you're the only one we haven't heard from."

"I'm here because you asked me along," I answered, trying to avoid sharing.

"John was always at my sister's coffee shop. I think he had the hots for her!" Danny laughed.

"What??" I objected. "We were just friends!" I could feel my face getting red.

"Oh, come on, John! Everyone in that shop knew you liked her, except maybe you!"

Now everyone was laughing. If it hadn't been so true, I might have been laughing with them.

Danny slapped me on the back, "It's ok buddy. You can just tell everyone how I saved your life!"

I looked him in the eye, smiling. "Maybe you should tell it."

"Ok! You see, there was this great big guy, and he had John on the floor with a gun pointed in his face, when I burst in the room and jumped on him!" Danny went on telling the story, adding several embellishments along the way, until he had everyone laughing.

The rest of the trip went by quickly with some times of chatting and laughter and some times of silence. We pulled in a long driveway and Bill said, "Here it is, home sweet home!"

As we rounded a bend, we got our first look at our new "home". It was a large, two-story white house with a wraparound porch. There were two large red barns with fencing around one. I supposed that was the cow barn. Off to one side was a large chicken coop. A couple of chocolate labs came running up to the van, barking. I checked on Muffin, who was in her crate by my feet. She looked pretty freaked out. "Don't worry, I'll take care of you," I whispered softly to her.

Bill parked in front of the house and a young man came out of the door to greet us. This must be the nephew we heard about. He ran out to the van and gave Janet a big hug.

"I was sooo worried about you two!" he exclaimed. I've been trying to call you for over a week, but I could never get through!"

"I'm sorry!" Janet cried. "We tried to call you too! We have a lot to talk about."

Bill introduced Jamie to us as we all got out. He looked a little confused and Bill laughed and said, "You always said you wanted a big family, so we brought you one!"

Everyone helped unpack and we carried our things inside. There was a small foyer that led into a large living room with a big fireplace that wrapped around into a spacious dining/kitchen area.

"There are four bedrooms upstairs," said Janet. "Danny and Luke can share and the rest of you each have your own." She led the way and we all grabbed our luggage and followed. Danny and Luke took the big room on the end that had two twin beds in it. I took the next one, it was small but had a nice big bed and small closet. Katie told Megan to take the next one and she took the one on the other end of the hall.

Janet said, "Why don't you get unpacked and I'll go make some dinner."

I took my duffel bag into my room and shut the door. This didn't feel real. This morning I was fighting for my life, now I had a nice room all to myself. I didn't know how you were supposed to pray, but I stopped and said, "Thank you, Lord." I unpacked my bag, using the small dresser and closet. The picture of Elle and her mom went on my nightstand. I had left Muffin downstairs, so I went down to ask Janet if it was ok if she stayed in my room. I didn't want her to have to go outside with the dogs. When I got down there Janet had already set up Muffin in the spacious laundry room with a basket and soft blanket, her bowls, and litter box.

"Just for now," Janet said, "until she gets used to the place, then she can roam the house." Of course, Janet would have a soft spot for animals—just like she did for lost people.

Dinner was a simple meal of sloppy joes and fresh green beans, but it was seriously the best meal I could remember. To celebrate she even made chocolate chip cookies. After we ate, Bill had the men go out to the barn with him and the girls helped Janet clean up.

"We're all going to have to chip in on the chores," Bill said. "Has anyone worked on a farm before?" We all shook our heads no. "Ok," he said with a sigh, "training starts now." I had no idea how much work a farm was! Cows had to be fed and milked, stalls cleaned, chickens fed, and eggs picked up. It was mid-October, so the garden was at its end with the exception of some pumpkins and other funny looking things I couldn't name. Bill had gotten most of his fields of corn harvested and his silos were full. "Workday starts at 4:00 am tomorrow boys," Bill said with a smile. Luke threw down his ball cap and jokingly said, "I'm going back to the city!" Everyone chuckled.

They also had two horses in the barn. "Does anyone ride?" Bill asked.

We all shook our heads no and then someone said, "I do." It was Megan. She walked up to the stall and started stroking the horse. He nuzzled her fondly.

"That's Kahn, and the other one is Seneca," Bill told her. "I can saddle them up tomorrow after chores if you want."

"I'd love to take care of them; that could be my part of the chores!" Megan begged.

"Ok, we'll go over everything in the morning," agreed Bill.

We headed back to the house well past dark. It was only 8:00 pm, but I was exhausted. I said good night and went up to my room. There was a decent sized bathroom on our end of the hall for the men and the girls shared a bathroom between their bedrooms. I was the first one upstairs, so thought I'd use it before anyone else came up. I took a quick shower and decided to shave. Have you ever looked in a mirror and not recognized the person starring back at you? That is what it felt like as I was shaving. My life had changed so much in 10 days. I finished up and went to bed. My mind kept replaying the events that led me here. There was sadness, but mostly I was just grateful.

CHAPTER 9

Welcome to Farm Life

A T 4:00 am my phone alarm went off. I got dressed and went downstairs. Janet had a pot of coffee brewed and was making pancakes and eggs. Katie was in the kitchen helping her.

"Good morning!" said Janet and handed me a cup of coffee. "Sit down and help yourself to breakfast." She had to be the cheeriest person I ever met, especially at 4:00 am!

"Thank you," I muttered and sat down.

The others came downstairs and joined us. Jamie's room was on the ground floor next to Bill and Janet's. He sat down and said, "This is great, I won't have to spend all day out in the barn!"

"You did a fine job taking care of everything while we were gone," Bill chuckled.

We finished breakfast and headed outside. Katie stayed in with Janet to help with the inside work. There was a bit of a chill in the air this morning. I wished I'd grabbed my other sweatshirt.

Bill said, "Luke, can you go take care of the chickens? John, Danny, and I will start with the cows. Jamie, can you show Megan how to feed and clean the horses?" We all went to our tasks. First, we fed the cows, then four of them had to be milked, then stalls cleaned.

"I don't believe there is anything nastier than a cow's stall!" I said, trying not to gag.

Bill belly-laughed. "You ain't seen nothin' yet!"

Just then we heard screaming coming from the chicken coop. We all dropped what we were doing and ran out there. Luke was being chased around the yard by a big rooster! We all laughed so hard we almost fell down.

It took us most of the morning to finish everything. We dragged ourselves back in the house and cleaned up for lunch. Janet showed Katie how to make fresh bread and we had sandwiches with cheese and ham and some canned peaches from their peach trees.

Katie seemed to be enjoying learning from Janet. "I thought food came from restaurants, not people's kitchens," she joked. Her eyes were sparkling, and she looked well rested. I was so glad she came along.

After lunch we sat in the living room listening to the satellite radio. The news was still pretty bleak. The government had started food rations and there were mile long lines of people waiting. Violence was common in the lines because the food would run out before the line did. If you could find something to buy, chances were you couldn't afford it as inflation was out of control. We were all very depressed after listening for a while.

Danny walked over to an old upright piano in the corner and started playing. My look of shock amused him. "I have talents you know nothing about!" he laughed. The song he was playing was vaguely familiar, but I couldn't remember what it was until Janet started singing "Amazing Grace, how sweet the sound that saved a wretch like me . . . " Some joined in. Others, like me, just enjoyed listening. When he finished playing, he said, "I did grow up in the church; I just wasn't smart enough to pay attention." I was kind of glad he hadn't.

That evening after supper, I asked who wanted to cut my stitches out. It was starting to itch like crazy and they looked mostly healed. Everyone gathered around me as I unwrapped it. Luke and Danny both said, "no way" and went to the other room. Janet went and got her sewing kit and produced a small scissors. She gave them to Bill, but his fingers were too big to fit the small holes. Katie took them and said she would try. Janet poured some alcohol over them. I jumped as Katie stuck me in the arm, trying to get the scissors under the first stitch. "I'm so sorry, John, but I can't get under them!"

Janet grabbed a small tweezer out of the case and poured more alcohol on it. "I'll try pulling them up so you can get under them, Katie. John, you're going to have to hold still!" I tried to brace myself as Janet pulled and Katie snipped. It must have looked pretty comical because pretty soon Danny and Luke were back in the kitchen watching and laughing. They had about half of them out when I had to take a break.

"This is worse than getting stabbed!" I said, shaking my arm a little. I sat back down and gritted my teeth, nodding for them to continue. They pulled and snipped some more until they were finally out.

I always thought I was in pretty good shape, but three days into farm chores I could barely move. Every muscle was sore. And I wasn't alone; every one of us "city folk" had trouble getting out of bed and walking down the stairs. Bill and Jamie just chuckled at us. We all got lessons on how to split wood with an axe. That was something I really enjoyed doing, but I got huge blisters at first. Katie had to cut the dead skin off for me. She was getting pretty good with those little scissors.

Our days drifted by with chores morning and evening, and the afternoons mostly for whatever we wanted. Muffin had settled in nicely and had free roam of the house. She was turning into a good mouser and would bring us her 'presents' when she caught them.

One afternoon, Megan wanted to go riding.

"I've never been on a horse," I told her, as I watched her saddle him up.

"Come with me!" she said. "Seneca is very easy to ride!"

Bill came walking in. "You should go, John!"

"Ok, but No Running!" I warned. I had watched her galloping around the pasture before.

"I promise!" she smiled. She saddled up both horses and walked them out of the barn. I watched her get on Kahn. Bill held Seneca's reins while I got on.

That wasn't so hard.

I got quick instructions on how to use the reins and Bill handed them to me.

"We'll just walk around the edge of the woods," she gave a little kick. Fortunately, Seneca was happy to walk wherever Kahn went, so I mostly just sat there. It was nice feeling the power of a horse underneath me.

"I can see why you like to ride," I told Megan. She took that as an invitation for speed.

"Let's try a trot!" and she kicked a little. Kahn responded and Seneca was right behind him. I was bouncing all over in the saddle.

"Put some weight on your feet in the stirrups! It will be a smoother ride!" I did, and she was right.

Then she kicked again and we were galloping slowly down the field. She looked at me to make sure I was ok. Just then a deer ran out of the woods and spooked both horses. Megan easily got Kahn back under control, but I had no clue! Seneca was in a full gallop, headed straight back to the barn. Megan took off after me. Kahn was the faster of the two and caught up quickly.

"Pull back on the reins!" she screamed at me. I was busy holding on to the saddle horn, trying not to fall off.

"Use the reins!" she yelled again. I tried to let go with one hand to pull back, but dropped one rein in the process. Megan steered Kahn right next to Seneca's head and grabbed her halter, then slowed Kahn, slowing us in the process.

"Are you alright? I'm so sorry!"

"I'm fine! I'm fine!" I assured her, as I got off Seneca. "I'll just walk back to the barn, if that's ok."

Megan smiled at me, "I'll get the horses."

Now I know why cowboys walk like they do.

We had been lucky with the electricity. It only went out a few times and Bill had a small generator we would use just to keep the refrigerator and freezer going. We had been chopping wood for the fireplace, so we didn't use any extra fuel on the furnace. We were reading the Bible and having 'church' on Sundays. Danny was our piano player. I was surprised by how many old hymns he could play from memory. Sometimes when the internet worked, we could bring up a YouTube video of a pastor giving a message. We took turns reading Revelation, looking for signs of what was to come. None of us really understood it, but we knew there was going to be someone called 'the antichrist' who would make things better for a while and then bad for anyone who wouldn't worship him as god.

Our gas situation wasn't critical, but we decided to go into the next town to see if anyone was selling it, or if we could siphon any more from abandoned cars. Bill had an assortment of hunting rifles and handguns. He wore a handgun in a holster and put two shotguns in the back seat "just in case". Danny, Bill, and I piled in the small car leaving Luke, Jamie, and the girls at the farm. It was about a 20 minute drive. As we drove into town, people starred at us; it gave me an eerie feeling. We stopped at a local gas station and mini mart. There were people there, but we learned they weren't selling any gas, or anything else. They asked where we were from.

Bill said, "Up the highway a ways," trying to be vague.

"Are you expecting any gas soon?" I asked the big guy standing next to me. He looked at me like I had just asked the dumbest question in the world.

Sarcastically he said, "Yeah, the president is sending a truck over right now!"

A small group of guys had gathered around the car.

"Where are you getting your gas?" one asked. We knew we needed to get out of there, but they had surrounded the car.

"I had a little bit left on the farm," Bill said.

Too much information . . . I walked up to the group of men, "We'll get out of your way" and tried to walk through them, expecting a fight. I was surprised when they stepped aside. Bill and Danny both got in and we left, quickly.

"I thought I was going to have to save your hide again!" Danny laughed nervously.

"Let's not do this again," said Bill. "I think we're on our own now." We all agreed.

We went straight back to the farm. There were no abandoned cars along the way, so we came back empty handed. We told the group what had happened. Janet said, "No more going to town, Bill! That could have ended very badly." She acted mad but gave him a big hug.

We got all the evening chores done and sat in the living room around the fire discussing how we could ration the gas even more. We had mostly used it on the generator when the power went out. We still had about 50 gallons in the 100 gallon tank. It was getting late, so I went up to bed and the others were right behind me.

At 2:00 am I heard the dogs barking. I turned the hall light on and was heading down the stairs when Danny joined me. Bill was already up looking steadily out the front window.

"I think there's someone out there," he whispered. Danny and I both peered out the window. It was cloudy so there was no moon or star light to see by. There was one light in the yard, but we couldn't see anyone there. I noticed Bill had his pistol.

"Go to the gun case and get a gun," he instructed quietly. Danny and I hurried to the case in the back hall and each grabbed a rifle.

"Go wake up the girls and tell them to get in the cellar. Get Luke and Jamie in here. Don't turn any lights on!" Danny got Luke and Jamie and I got the girls. I turned the hall light off, knocked lightly, and cracked the door.

"You need to get up and come downstairs. Don't turn any lights on, someone is out there." Then I went to Megan's door and repeated that. When we got downstairs, Janet was waiting with a pistol and took the girls down to the cellar.

Bill looked at Janet, "See if you can bolt the door."

"Please be careful," Janet whispered and disappeared down the stairs with the girls.

The dogs were still barking but we couldn't see anyone.

"Two of us need to go check on the gas tank." Bill looked at us.

"I will," I said.

Bill explained his plan. "We'll slip out the back door, it's darker back there. Jamie, you watch the front door. Luke, watch the back. Danny, see if you can slip into the barn. You might have a better view from the loft." Luke and Jamie posted themselves at the doors. They each had a pistol. Bill, Danny, and I slipped out the back into the black night. Danny headed towards the barn while I followed Bill towards gas tank. The dogs had quit barking. My heart was racing and my breath was coming in short gasps. I wondered if the guys from town had found us. I saw Danny slip in the barn door. Bill and I ran to the machine barn and silently crept around it. The gas tank was on the back side of the barn. I thought I could see movement near the tank. Suddenly a shot rang out. They must have seen us! As I raised my rifle, Bill pulled it down hard.

"You can't shoot at the gas tank!" he hissed. He was right; I hadn't thought of that! We took cover on the side of the barn. Danny must have known not to shoot towards the tank because there was no return fire.

Bill whispered, "I'm going to creep up the tree line and see if I can get a better look. Go check on Danny." I nodded and watched him head off towards the trees. Then I crept back the way we came and went towards the cattle barn. I stopped for a minute to listen for any noises. Would I really shoot someone? I prayed I wouldn't have to find out. I got to the door of the barn and slipped in.

"Danny?" I said softly. "Danny, it's me."

I didn't want to get shot by him. The darkness was thick in there. All of a sudden, he touched my shoulder.

"It's me," he said as I jumped out of my skin.

I grabbed his shoulder, wanting to punch him for the scare, but really just happy he was ok.

"I can't see anything from here," he told me.

"Bill went down the tree line to get a better look. Maybe we can sneak through the pasture and get closer."

Danny nodded and we crept quietly back out the door. As we made our way through the pasture, we could hear voices in the distance. I couldn't make out what they were saying though. The clouds were moving out and the moon shed its light on the scene. We both dropped to the ground as we watched three men fill gas cans from the tank and put them in the back of a truck. I couldn't tell if there was someone in the truck. We laid there watching, not sure what to do. I didn't see Bill anywhere. It looked like they were finishing up. Danny and I looked at each other. We knew if we just let them drive off, they would keep coming back. We crept on our stomachs to get closer. As they were loading their last cans into the truck, Bill stepped out from behind the tank pointing his gun at them.

"Hold it right there!" he yelled.

Danny and I jumped up and yelled, "Hands up!"

We all had our guns trained on the three men as we walked closer. The men put the gas cans down and their hands up. I recognized them from the gas station.

"Put your hands on the truck and keep them there!" Bill ordered. He was stepping up to pat them down when I heard the unmistakable sound of a rifle cock and felt a jab in my back.

"Unless you want your buddy to have a big hole in his chest, you better drop 'em!" someone hollered.

Where did this guy come from? My mind raced trying to find another option, but I dropped my gun, as did Danny and Bill. The other three guys grabbed them up and pointed them at us. The one with his rifle in my back shoved me towards Bill and motioned for Danny to follow.

"What are we going to do now?" asked one of the guys while another one patted us down.

"How many people live here?" the tall guy asked.

"It's just us," said Bill.

The guy with the rifle walked over to him and then slammed the butt of his gun in Bill's face.

"You better not be lying to me!"

Bill reeled back but stayed on his feet.

"He's not lying!" I yelled.

The guy walked over to me. I braced myself, but all he said was, "Let's find out," and he motioned for us to move towards the house.

Blood was pouring out of Bill's nose as we slowly walked back towards the house. I prayed that Jamie and Luke were watching. When we got to the front porch, they told us to stop.

"Down on your knees!" We all had guns shoved into our backs, so we kneeled.

My heart was pounding, and my mind was racing.

"There's no one else here!" I yelled, hoping they would hear inside.

Rifle man's foot slammed into my chest, sending me backwards to the ground. He stepped on my neck. I was struggling to get him off, gasping for air.

"Just take what you want and go!" yelled Danny.

The guy took his foot off me and looked at the house. "If you're in there and you care what happens to your friends, you better come out!"

Please Lord, don't let them come out.

There was no movement inside, so after a few minutes he sent one of the other guys in to check it out. Bill, Danny and I glanced at each other. After a few minutes a light switched on in the house and the guy hollered out, "It looks empty!"

Rifle man told us all to go inside. We went in and I wondered where the others had gone. Maybe the cellar . . . He lined up three chairs in the kitchen and told us all to sit. I was looking for a chance to fight, but there were always at least two guns trained on us. I couldn't take the risk.

The guy I named 'rifle man' was going through the cabinets, I supposed looking for food, but came over to me and said, "Where's your rope?"

"It's all out in the barn."

He wasn't really happy with that and started throwing things out of the drawers. He found some extension cords and calmed down a bit.

"These will do!" He threw them to the other two guys that were behind us.

"Tie them to the chair!" he ordered.

Once we were tied, the two that had kept their guns on us relaxed and started looking around the kitchen. The fourth guy had been upstairs and when he came down said, "There's no one up there."

I was testing the strength of the cord. It didn't feel like I would be able to break out of it.

Danny said, "Look, you can have the gas and take the food, whatever you want, just take it and go!"

"W e l l, that's real nice of you son," drawled rifle man, walking over towards Danny. He grabbed him by the hair and jerked his head back, staring him in the face. Fear and anger rose in me as I struggled harder with the cords around my wrists. He jerked Danny's head forward and then let him go.

The four of them went to the other side of the kitchen and started talking. I couldn't catch it all, but they were discussing what to do with us. I glanced at Bill and Danny. We knew we were in trouble if the others didn't show up soon. Just then I saw Luke looking out of the hall closet. He was trying to tell me something. The best I could figure was he needed a distraction. I looked at Bill and Danny to see if they had seen him. They had.

"Look fellas," I said. "I'm sure we can work something out."

Bill piped in "Yes, nobody has to get hurt here."

"Right," said Danny. "Come over here and we can negotiate!"

They laughed at that, but it worked. They all walked over and stood in front of our chairs. They had all set their guns down, with the exception of rifle man.

"Ok!" taunted one guy, "start negotiating!" and they all laughed.

That was what we needed. With one orchestrated effort we lunged at them, chair and all, knocking two of them down as we crashed to the floor. The fall had broken Danny's chair and he was free, wrestling with one of the men on the floor. Luke and Jamie came flying out of the closet hollering "freeze!" The two men closest to us lunged at them, grabbing their gun hands. A shot rang out as they struggled. I had to get free, so I managed to get on my feet and slammed myself into the big kitchen bar, trying to break the chair. I felt it crack so I did it again. This time it worked and I quickly untangled myself from the broken chair and cord. Rifle man had raised his gun and aimed it at the mass of struggling bodies, but there was no clear shot. He was on the other side of the bar and I was pretty sure hadn't seen me get loose, so I stayed low and hurried around it. His attention was on the chaos when I sprang out and grabbed him, trying to knock the gun away. It worked—the gun fell on the counter as we both fell to the floor. This guy was big and punched hard. He landed one on my chin that almost sent me reeling, but I managed to get him in a bear hug and hung on, trying to clear my head. I could hear the others still fighting and the sound of another chair breaking.

That must be Bill.

Rifle man was trying to get up to get to his rifle, dragging me with him, so I punched him as hard as I could in the stomach. It stopped him for a second, but he landed another punch on my jaw and I couldn't hang on.

As I fell, I saw Bill grab him just as he picked up his rifle. A shot rang out and I saw Danny spin around and fall. Then another shot rang out. Janet was in the kitchen with her gun raised and I saw rifle man fall. All the fighting had stopped, and Janet was pointing her pistol at the remaining three robbers. Jamie and Luke grabbed the closest guns and pointed them at the intruders. Bill went over to Janet, took her gun, and they stood locked in each other's arms. Megan and Katie came out of the cellar.

I crawled over to Danny. He was face down, not moving.

"Danny?" I gently turned him over. There was a pool of blood underneath him.

"We have to get him to the hospital!" I yelled.

Bill came over and checked his pulse while Janet got a large towel and applied pressure to the wound.

He moaned a little and she said, "You're going to be ok, Danny. We're taking you to the hospital right now."

Jamie and Luke had tied up the other three men. I looked at Luke and then rifle man, who was laying lifeless on the floor. Luke shook his head no. Bill grabbed the car keys and brought it around to the door. He and I carefully carried Danny out to the car and laid him in the back seat. I got in with him and kept pressure on his wound, which made him moan again. I prayed that was a good sign. As Bill was getting in the car, he told Janet he would send the police out as soon as he could, and he hit the gas. I pleaded with God the whole way to spare Danny's life.

We finally pulled up to the emergency room and Bill ran in. Two EMT guys came running out with a stretcher. I got out of their way as they checked him out and quickly wheeled him into the hospital. It was like a scene from TV . . . they rushed him in, hooked up IV's, then took him in the elevator. Bill and I stood there, helpless.

Bill asked if he could use the hospital's land line to call the police and a nurse led us to a waiting room with a phone. He called and gave them the address and told them the story, letting them know he would be at the hospital. After about 20 minutes a doctor came in to talk to us. They were taking Danny into surgery now. He sounded hopeful that no major organs had been hit. Bill and I prayed together for Danny, and the surgeon.

After six grueling hours of waiting a nurse finally came in. "Danny's in recovery. The surgery went well but you won't be able to see him for a while, why don't you go home."

It was after noon and we knew everyone at the house would be worried.

"When will we be able to see him?" I questioned.

"Why don't you come back in the morning."

As we drove back home Bill said, "Everyone is going to learn how to use the guns, and we need to start a watch at night. I can make up a schedule." When we pulled up to the house everyone came spilling out the door, wanting to know how Danny was.

"He's stable right now. They said we could see him tomorrow." I answered.

Janet told how the police had made it out about two hours after we left as we all went back inside.

"Bill, why don't you and John come and eat something? We saved you some lunch," Janet told us as she got two plates from the refrigerator.

As we ate Bill said, "We are going to take some shooting lessons, I want everyone in this house to know how to use the guns. Also, I think we need to start a night watch. I could make a schedule where we each have a few hours through the night."

"Bill, don't we still have those solar motion detector flood lights?" questioned Janet.

"I think we do! I'll check in the attic."

"He's always buying stuff we 'need' and then not using it." She shook her finger at Bill.

"I knew we'd need those some day!" He put his plate in the sink and went upstairs to look.

"I'm going to go upstairs and clean up," I said, as I set my plate in the sink also. Luke followed me upstairs and stopped at my bedroom door.

"So, Danny's gonna be ok, right?" he asked me.

"The doctor said there was no major organ damage – yeah, I'm sure he'll be fine," I replied, trying to convince myself too.

"I want to go with you tomorrow, back to the hospital." He was staring me in the eyes.

"Of course."

Bill came down with a large box. "I found them! Let's take them outside and set them up so the sun can power up the batteries."

Luke and I followed him downstairs. Jamie came out with us too, and Bill instructed us as to where to put them. When we got back in the house, Janet, Katie, and Megan were working on a night watch schedule. None of us wanted to be surprised by night visitors again.

The next morning after chores Bill took us all out to the edge of the woods. He set up some tin cans on stumps for target practice. I had taken a concealed carry class a few years ago, so I was pretty confident in my shooting ability, but it had been a while since I shot a gun. It took me a few shots, but I finally hit the can. We didn't want to waste too much ammunition so those who shot a lot, like Bill and Jamie, instructed the girls. I was impressed at how quickly they learned how to load and shoot.

After lunch Luke and I headed to the hospital. Danny was still in ICU, so only one person could go in at a time. I let Luke go first and when he came out, I thought maybe something had happened! He sat down next to me with his face in his hands, crying. I put my hand on his shoulder and started to run into the ICU room. He grabbed my arm and pulled me back.

"He's Ok! He's Ok! I just wasn't ready to see him hooked up to all those things. This whole nightmare just caught up with me."

I sat with him till he gained his composure, then went in to see Danny. He had tubes coming out of everywhere, and three IV bags going into him. He wasn't awake so I just sat there next to him.

A nurse came in and I asked, "Is he ok?"

"He's stable for now." She checked the monitor to make sure everything was well.

"How come he's not awake?" I wondered.

"It's normal for him to sleep a lot after this kind of surgery. And he is heavily sedated."

She finished checking all his tubes and left. I went back out to check on Luke and told him what the nurse had said. He wanted to go back in and sit with him, in case he did wake up, so I stayed in the waiting room. They had coffee in there, so I helped myself to some, then found some old magazines in a rack and killed time looking at them. About half an hour later Luke came out and told me he was awake and said I should go in. When I went in the room, he was staring at the ceiling. I went up to the bed so he could see me. His eyes caught mine and he raised his eyebrows a little, then weakly lifted his hand to grab mine. I gently squeezed his hand and said, "Hey! You're going to be fine! The doctor said so. You'll be home in a few weeks!" Danny let go of my hand and drifted off to sleep again. I sat in the room a few more minutes, praying for healing for Danny and then went back out to Luke. We decided to head home so we could help with night chores since Danny was sleeping.

That evening at supper we discussed our gas shortage and how we were going to be able to get to and from the hospital. Everyone knew we would not be able to keep driving there every day, so we decided to wait two days and then go back, hoping Danny would be more awake. And we would bring him some pajamas and clothes and see what else he needed.

Bill ran a few 'night alarms' so we all knew what to do in case of another attack. The solar lights worked pretty well. We got to see lots of deer and fox in their light, but thankfully, no people.

Luke and I headed back to the hospital two days later. Danny had been moved out of ICU and put in a private room. We walked in and he was awake and alert. Still hooked up to several tubes, but he looked so much better!

"You look good!" I grinned.

Danny just smiled weakly, "Your standards aren't very high, are they?"

Luke unpacked his clothes and pajamas that we brought and put them in the drawer. He held up the pajama bottoms and said, "For when you can walk down the hall!"

Danny moaned, "No jokes!" as he tried not to laugh.

We explained to him that we could not use the gas to come see him every day but would try to get there every three or four days.

"Do you need anything?" Luke asked him.

He sighed. "I just need to go home."

"I know buddy, I know. Soon! Just get better." Luke patted his leg.

We stayed the afternoon and then left about supper time.

CHAPTER 10

Thanksgiving

T HANKSGIVING was just a week away and we were hoping Danny would be released soon. He was doing well with his PT and the doctor said if he continued to improve in the next few days, he would discharge him so he could celebrate at home. Bill and Jamie had been out hunting wild turkey, but hadn't gotten one yet. We moved Jamie upstairs with Luke so Danny could have the downstairs bedroom for a while.

It was the Wednesday before Thanksgiving when Luke and I went back to the hospital. Danny was dressed and packed up, waiting to see the doctor one last time. We sat with him for about an hour until finally the doctor came in. He explained everything Danny should and should not be doing and then the nurse wheeled him to the exit. I had gone to get the car and was waiting for them out front. Luke helped him in the front seat and we headed home.

When we got there, Bill and Jamie were cleaning a large turkey they had just shot. Everyone came out and welcomed Danny home, fussing over him. He was all smiles, as were the rest of us.

It was Thanksgiving day. The turkey was in the oven and Janet and Katie went all out with the sides. Mashed potatoes, gravy, green beans, even cornbread stuffing, with pumpkin pie for dessert. Megan and Jamie were setting the table; they seemed to be together a lot. Bill and Luke were playing chess.

"Checkmate!" hollered Luke.

We all laughed as Bill pretended to be mad; he hadn't beaten Luke yet.

"Come and get it!" hollered Janet.

Everyone made their way to the table, raving about how good it looked.

"Do you need a hand?" I asked, looking at Danny on the couch.

He shook his head, "No, I got it," but I went over anyway and put my hand out.

Danny looked up and gratefully accepted. He had spent three weeks in the hospital and we had some scares, but he was home now. We all sat down, held hands, and gave thanks. As I watched the scene at the table, I said my own prayer of thanks silently. I remembered Elle and imagined her sitting here with us, laughing at Luke's silly jokes. It was my love for her that led me to Danny, and Danny led me to this group. Elle once said she wasn't sure why God led her to the coffee shop.

It was for me Elle . . . it was for all of us.

Someday I would get to tell her that.

CHAPTER 11

Secret Santa

W HEN I walked in the house Friday after morning chores, it looked like Christmas had thrown up in every room. There were garlands, lights, trees, and ornaments everywhere!

Bill walked in, "Here we go! I should have warned you about what happens every Friday after Thanksgiving."

Janet heard us come in. "Bill, there's more boxes in the barn loft, can you get them?"

"I can give you hand," I offered, walking back outside with him. "She really loves Christmas, huh?"

"You don't know the half of it!" Bill chuckled. "She told me now that she knows the real meaning of Christmas, she is more excited than ever to decorate."

The Labs came running up. We never did figure out what happened to them the night of the robbery. They showed up two days later looking no worse for the wear.

Bill said, "She usually puts lights all down the driveway, but I think we'll keep them inside this year," and winked at me.

I looked at his broken nose and agreed. We all told him it gave his face more character. He climbed into the loft and handed down two large boxes. We carried them into the house and placed them in the middle of the mess. Danny was even helping out; he was in the recliner trying to untangle several strings of lights.

Janet said, "I tell Bill every year if he would wind those back up neatly when he puts them away, we wouldn't have this mess!"

Bill hung his head, "It's true." We all laughed.

"Here's one!" piped Danny, as he freed one strand from the tangled ball.

"John, can you help me hang this garland?" Katie called from the hallway.

"I'm coming!" I hollered, as I made my way towards the stair railing that she was working on.

I wound the garland around the banister, following her instructions, as we made our way up the stairs.

She touched my arm and said, "Thanks."

I smiled down at her and our eyes locked. She held the gaze for a few seconds but then I looked away.

"I better change out of these work clothes," I muttered and I slipped into my bedroom. I didn't know why I always felt so awkward with her.

When I went back down to the living room, there were two tall artificial trees needing decorating; one by the front window and one by the dining room table. Megan and Jamie were working on the one in the dining room, so I went over to the one in the living room. Katie had gone into the kitchen to help get lunch ready. Bill and Luke were hanging garland in all the doorways, so I pulled a chair up to the tree and said, "Danny, put that mess down and come help me!" He slowly got out of the recliner and walked over to the chair. I handed him a box of ornaments.

"You take those out and hand them to me." He complied without comment.

"Are you feeling ok?" I asked him quietly.

"I'm alright, I just need some time to heal."

"Take all the time you need," I said with a smile.

He smiled back. "I'm really just trying to get out of the chores!" he said loud enough for everyone to hear.

"Next time just tell me!" Bill hollered. "You didn't have to get shot!"

"Don't make me laugh!" moaned Danny, holding his side.

Janet called, "Lunch is ready!"

I helped Danny out of his chair and we made our way to the table. It was meatless spaghetti with homemade sauce and rolls. We held hands and gave thanks. After lunch Danny went over to the piano and played some Christmas carols while we finished the decorations.

I had never had a Christmas like this. As a boy I was lucky to get a tree with one gift under it.

"Why don't we do secret Santa gifts?" Katie suggested. "We can draw names and then you have to make a gift to give that person Christmas morning!"

The girls thought it was awesome, the boys just stared at each other.

"Come on! It will be fun!" Janet pleaded. She wrote everyone's name on a slip of paper and put them in a bowl. Then she went around the room saying, "Draw one name and don't tell who you get!"

We all took a slip of paper out.

"I got myself—this should be easy!" Luke shouted.

"Put it back!" ordered Janet. "If you draw yourself you have to put it back!"

We drew until everyone had a different name. I got Katie. My heart started to pound a little.

What is the deal, John!

It wasn't that I didn't like her, but I felt so awkward and self-conscious when it was just the two of us. I shoved the paper in my pocket.

I decided to go out and chop some firewood. There was a strong north wind blowing. Bill thought we might be in for some snow soon. I enjoyed chopping wood, it gave me a chance to be alone for a bit. Don't get me wrong, I was eternally grateful for these people. Each one was family to me, but having been alone most of my life I sometimes needed a break. It was chilly outside, but I worked up a sweat so, I took off my outer shirt. My mind drifted to Bill and Janet. They weren't a couple I would have put together. Bill was a mountain of a man, close to six feet with a build to match, and Janet wasn't much more than five feet, but they could read each other like a book. They fussed at each other but never really fought. I wondered what it would be like to grow up in that kind of home.

It's too bad they couldn't have children, they would have been great parents.

Katie came outside with a heavy coat on. "Aren't you freezing?"

"No! The temperature is just right!" I said back, grinning.

"John, I need a piece of wood," she said as she walked around looking at the scrap pieces; the smaller branches scattered about. "I have an idea for my secret Santa."

I picked up some sticks and said, "Like these?"

"No, it needs to be . . . thicker, with several branches connected."

I raised an eyebrow at her.

"You know, like a spot where the tree shot out branches!"

Using her hands, she tried to show me what she wanted. I laughed out loud.

"John! You know what I mean!" she scolded, holding in her own laughter.

I walked around picking up pieces of tree, showing them to her.

"That one!" she shouted.

"Someone's going to be very lucky."

She playfully glared at me, "At least I have an idea!" and she went back in the house.

"True," I muttered under my breath and went back to chopping wood.

When I had everything stacked, I carried in an arm load to put by the fireplace.

"Wow! The house looks great!" I complimented.

"I only wish I had a nativity. That's the one thing missing," Janet mused.

Megan said, "It looks like the Hallmark movies I used to watch!"

"I loved those movies!" Katie exclaimed.

Then all the girls were chatting about which movie was their favorite and who the best leading man was. I rolled my eyes and went upstairs to change clothes again. I sat down on my bed. I couldn't believe that in the middle of the world collapsing God had given me the family I'd always wanted. I was overwhelmed by His grace . . . and so thankful.

Chapter 12

The Skunk

Two days later it started to snow fast and heavy. We were like little kids and ran outside. The snow fell all morning and by lunch we had several inches on the ground. After we ate, Bill went out to the shed and came back in with two toboggans.

"Who's game?" he challenged.

Luke said, "I am!"

Danny pretended to pout. "You all go on, I'll just stay here by myself . . . "

"You can get the hot cocoa ready—and don't forget the marshmallows!" Luke told him and winked.

I couldn't remember the last time I tried to toboggan down a hill, but I got bundled up, along with everyone else, and headed to the hill in the backyard. It was a good-sized hill that went down into a small gully. There were several trees at the bottom, so we looked for the best spot.

"Let's try it here!" shouted Luke and he grabbed one of the sleds. He took it down by himself the first time.

Bill looked at Janet, "Should we try it?"

"You betcha!" and they both squeezed onto a sled.

Jamie gave them a push down the hill and they crashed at the bottom, both laughing. Janet laid in the snow and made a snow angel. Luke brought the other sled back up and gave it to Jamie, and he and Megan went down together.

Jamie hollered, "We win!" as they had gone the farthest.

"Come on, John, let's show them how it's done!" Katie hollered, so we both piled on the sled.

Bill gave us a big push and we went flying down the hill. We passed Jamie's run and were still flying. I had no idea how to steer it and we were headed straight for a big tree.

"Abandon ship!" I yelled and tipped us both off. We went tumbling head over heels but missed the tree. "Are you ok?" I asked Katie, worried she had gotten hurt. She picked her head up and her face was covered with snow. Suddenly she grinned at me. Once I realized she was ok, I started to laugh, uncontrollably! She made a snowball and threw it at me, hitting me in the neck.

"Oh, it's on girl!" I hollered, and we had a good old fashioned snowball fight. Everyone joined in and we laughed like little kids until we were all exhausted. We trudged back to the house and made a mess in the foyer with all the snow.

"Where's that hot cocoa?" Luke asked Danny with a smile. Danny threw a sofa pillow at him.

Janet said, "Hot chocolate, coming up!"

That evening we listened to the news again. The countries were joining something called World Economic Organization. They were formulating a plan to get the world's economy going again. It seemed to be spearheaded from Saudi Arabia. They were also reporting that Los Angeles had a 6.5 earthquake. Several roads and buildings had been damaged. The death toll was not known at this time.

The next morning, I could barely get out of bed. I met Luke and Jamie in the hall, on our way down to breakfast, and they were both hobbling down the stairs as well. Everyone was moving slowly, complaining about how sore they were. Danny thought we were making fun of him when he came into the kitchen.

"I guess we really aren't kids anymore!" said Bill, and we laughed and moaned.

I put the last couple logs in the fireplace and went out to get more. The moon was shining bright in the early morning sky and the snow sparkled like diamonds.

"How beautiful, God!" I breathed. I had never noticed the beauty of His creation in my old life.

I brushed the snow off the wood pile. Just then the *most awful smell* enveloped me. I started gagging, trying to catch my breath. Then I saw a little skunk scurrying away in the snow. Still gagging, I tried rolling in the snow to get the smell off. It didn't seem to work. I went back up to the house and stepped in the foyer. "Oh My Gosh!" yelled Janet, "Go back outside!" Everyone was holding their noses and screaming at me to get out! I stepped back outside.

Now what?

Bill came out the door holding his nose, motioning for me to get off the porch. I went down and stood in the snow. He started laughing so hard he couldn't talk. I didn't see the humor as I stood there, still gagging a little. I could see everyone looking out the window at me, in the same state Bill was in, doubled over with laughter. Bill managed to croak out, "Go to the barn and strip off those clothes. Throw them out in the snow and we'll burn them. I'll bring you some new ones." He went back in and I could see everyone laughing even harder. I walked to the barn, still gagging, and stripped down to my birthday suit, then tossed everything outside. The smell was much better, but now I'm standing naked in a cold barn.

"Maybe I should have waited for the new set of clothes before I stripped," I said out loud. Then I started to laugh at the ridiculousness of this scene! "Come on Bill! I'm freezing!" I started jumping up and down, trying to stay warm.

Finally, I heard him coming. He was still laughing! He opened the door and threw my clothes and a towel at me. "There's a bucket of water and some lye soap over by the horses. Good luck!" Then started laughing even harder and left.

I am never going to live this down, I thought, as I scrubbed and pulled my clothes on.

I wondered if I could just live in the barn . . .

As I walked in the house everyone burst into laughter, again. I did my best version of a bow and let them get it out of their systems. Janet tried to tell me to come and eat, but she couldn't get the words out without more hysterical laughing. I sat down and tried to ignore them. Finally, everyone calmed down and we were getting ready to go do chores.

Danny said, "Hey, John, could you bring in some more wood?" and everyone was rolling on the floor again.

Danny moaned in pain from laughing and I shouted, "Serves you right!" and headed out the door. We made it through chores without too many outbursts of laughter. I had to admit, it was pretty funny.

The next few weeks flew by, and I still didn't have any idea what to make Katie for Christmas. I asked some of the guys what they were doing, but no one would tell me. I wondered if they were equally as stumped as I was. I went out to chop more wood. It was the only heat we had so we went through it pretty fast. I needed to go out to the woods and find some more trees that had fallen. I grabbed one of the sleds thinking I could pull the wood out with it. As I stomped through the snow, I gave myself a pep talk, "You've only got one week left, John! Think of something!" but nothing came to me.

I stopped thinking about it and concentrated on finding some good wood. We had already cleared out most of the fallen trees, so I had to walk pretty far into the woods before I found a couple good sized trees that were down. I chopped them into smaller pieces and piled them on the sled, tying them down with rope. *Maybe I piled it too high*, I thought as I tried to pull the sled . . . but didn't want to leave any behind, so I leaned into it. I had to stop several times to catch my breath.

Then it came to me! "I know what I can give her!"

That gave me new strength and I pulled the sled to the edge of the woods. Jamie saw me coming and ran out to help.

"Thanks!" I said as we both pulled together.

"You should have come and got me! Next time don't go alone!"

I slapped his back. "Good advice!"

CHAPTER 13

Christmas

WE decided not to listen to the news for a week before Christmas. Everything we heard on the radio was doom and gloom and there really was no good news to be had. So we just shut out the world and focused on our life on the farm.

Christmas was four days away and everyone seemed to be spending a lot more time alone in their rooms or out in the barn, I assumed trying to get their gifts ready. Janet suggested we write some kind of note with our gift. She also brought up several rolls of Christmas wrapping paper that she had accumulated and some tape. I wasn't good at notes. I could write up a story for a newscast, but when it came to expressing my emotions, I was at a loss for words. But I got something down on paper and wrapped up my gift. I snuck it under the tree early the next morning and saw there were two other gifts there. By Christmas Eve everyone had managed to slip their gifts under the tree unnoticed. After evening chores and dinner, we sat around the piano singing Christmas carols and Bill read the Christmas story out of the book of Matthew. Then we all went to bed.

Christmas morning doesn't mean we don't have chores, so we were all up at 4:00 am. Janet and Katie made a special breakfast of eggs, sausage, and hash browns, and were working on cinnamon rolls for later. As I headed out the door, I was questioning my gift.

She's going to think it's stupid, but it was too late now. We finished a little before lunch and went in to clean up.

Everyone was in the living room ready to open gifts. Katie suggested we get our gift from under the tree and hand it to whoever it was for, one at a time.

"Luke, why don't you start, and we'll go around the room," Janet suggested. Luke got up and picked up a rectangular present in Santa paper, then walked it over to Danny. Danny carefully opened the gift and studied what was inside for a minute before turning it around for everyone to see. It was a drawing of Danny and Luke in baseball uniforms, with their arms around each other's shoulders.

"Luke!" exclaimed Janet. "You drew that? I didn't know you were such a good artist!"

Danny said, "This is a copy of an old photograph of us back in high school! It's exactly like I remember it!"

"Beautiful!" said Janet, "Now read your note."

Danny looked at Luke and then started to read:

> *Danny,*
> *You were there when I needed someone on my side,*
> *and you gave me a home.*
> *You have been like a brother to me.*
> *Know that I will always be on your side.*
> *And please don't get shot again.*
> *Luke*

Everyone chuckled a little until Danny got up and went over to Luke and we watched them embrace each other. Then we were all fighting tears.

Danny was next in the circle so he went to get his present. I helped him pick it up so he wouldn't have to bend over, and he walked it over to Janet. Then he went over to the piano bench and sat down. Janet opened it. She looked at it and then at Danny. He motioned for her to bring it to him and then explained, "Read the note."

Dear Janet,

I don't know how to express how grateful I am for you. My mother died when I was young and I always felt a little cheated, until God put us together in that little church. You have become a mother, a mentor, and a friend to me. You gave us all a home when we needed it. You saved my life, in more ways than I can count. I know you love Christmas, so I wrote you this song.

Love Danny

Then Danny started to play a beautiful melody and sing:

"A baby in a manger
A star in the sky
An angel and a shepherd
It was no small thing.

Wisemen from afar
Gifts for a king
Angels rejoicing
It was no small thing

A virgin and an angel
A man and a dream
A journey on a donkey
It was no small thing

God's perfect gift to all who believe
Sent to bring us home
The perfect Lamb of God
Now seated on His throne

From the manger to the cross
With his arms open wide
How great the Father's love for us
It was no small thing"

Janet was crying now. She went over to Danny and hugged him for a long time. All of us were trying to hold it together. Katie picked up some tissues and passed them around.

When Janet finally sat down, it was Bill's turn. He got up and picked up a medium sized box wrapped in ornament paper and walked it over to Megan. She smiled at him and opened it. She looked a little confused and pulled out a horse halter.

Bill motioned for her to read the note:

> *Megan,*
>> *I am so thankful God sent you to us. I've watched how you have connected to Kahn, how he has helped heal your heart. Janet and I are so proud of the young lady you are becoming. Know that your parents would be proud of you too.*
>> *We love you,*
>> *Bill.*
>> *Kahn is yours.*

Megan's eyes became wide with surprise. "You mean I can keep him?" And she went over and gave Bill a hug, and then Janet.

Megan was next and she picked up a package and handed it to Luke. He unwrapped a plate of frosted cut out cookies. He bit into one, smiling, and read the note:

> *Luke,*
>> *I always wished I had a big brother, and if I did, I would want him to be you. I love your silly side. You always know when I need to laugh.*
>> *Love,*
>> *Megan*

Luke got up and gave her a hug saying, "You would have been a great little sis." Then messed up her hair. We all laughed.

"That's what big brothers do!" laughed Janet.

Janet was next in line. She picked up a small box wrapped in gold paper and handed it to Jamie. He unwrapped it and pulled out a heart ornament.

Then he read:

Dear Jamie,

Every time I look in your eyes, I see my brother staring back at me. When we took you in after the car accident, I was so unsure I could give you what you needed, but instead, you gave me what I needed. It's funny how we don't see God's hand on our lives until we look back and realize He was there all along. I am so proud of you.

You will always hold my heart.

Love,

Janet

They both got up and met each other with a big hug.

Jamie was next and handed his present to Bill. He opened the box and pulled out a picture of the farm house with a frame made of old barn wood. At the top was etched the word, Family.

He showed it to Janet and read the note:

Uncle Bill,

I don't know where to start. When my parents died, I was so scared that no one would take care of me. I remember feeling so lost when I moved in here, but you and Aunt Janet loved me through all those fears. You patiently put up with my temper tantrums, knowing my heart was broken and needed to mend. No matter how awful I treated you, you kept loving me. You are the best parents I could ask for and I love you both.

Jamie

The three of them were now in a group hug, crying.

I excused myself to the bathroom. I hadn't expected everyone's emotions to be so open. I had walled myself off for so long that I didn't know how to handle the honesty of everyone's feelings. I splashed some water on my face and went back out.

Katie was next in line, and I knew she and I were the only ones left that hadn't received a gift. My heart started pounding as she handed me the box. I was conscious of my hands shaking a little as I opened it. I pulled out a small carving of a horse with a knight sitting on its back. It was surprisingly good!

"So this is what the wood was for!" I said, smiling at her.

"Bill may have helped me with it," and she winked at him.

I read the note:

> *Dear John,*
>
> > *I didn't know you very well until we were put together
> > as a team at work. You were very quiet and didn't seem to
> > want to socialize, but as we worked together, I began to see
> > your heart of compassion for others; even strangers on the
> > street. I was so frightened after people started disappear-
> > ing, but tried not to show it. I think you knew though. You
> > stayed strong and made me feel safe . . . you even stole for
> > me! I was at the point of panic when you showed up at my
> > doorstep and gave me hope again. You helped point me to
> > Jesus. You are my 'Knight in shining armor'. Don't hide
> > your heart from others because it is beautiful.*
> >
> > *Love,*
> > *Katie*

I could barely finish the letter. She stood up and we hugged. I knew
I needed to be more honest with her when I handed her my gift.

"Before you open it, I'd like to say something," I continued,
addressing the whole group.

"I've never had a relationship where I was comfortable sharing my emotions. My dad didn't allow it, and I got pretty good at
pushing everything down. Being with you all has shown me that I
don't have to be so guarded all the time."

"Katie," I said, looking right at her, "somehow you remind me
of what I lost when Elle left, and that makes me want to hide. I feel
like sometimes I'm pushing your friendship away because I don't
know how to deal with the emotions those memories bring up. I
thank God for every one of you," I said, looking around the circle.

"I hope you all know that I love you. You are teaching me
what family is."

Tears were coming as I sat down and motioned for Katie to
open her gift. She carefully unwrapped the jar of canned peaches I
had wrapped, and read the note:

> *Dear Katie,*
> > *I promise I will never let you go hungry.*
> > *Love,*
> > *John*

Katie and I stood and hugged each other. Then everyone stood and we were all hugging, one giant ball of tangled arms and tears.

Chapter 14

The Hard Winter

J ANUARY was a hard month. The weather was brutal with below zero temps, ice storms, and a lot of snow and wind. We had cleared the woods of fallen trees and now had to use our ever dwindling supply of gasoline to run the chain saw to cut down trees for the fireplace. The axe worked to chop most of it but was not a good option for cutting them down. Every afternoon, after morning chores and lunch, we were back outside chopping wood, trying to stay ahead of the fireplace demand.

Gasoline was starting to get shipped into rural areas, and we were able to get the farm on a list for a tank refill, but there was no clear date when that might be. The weather did not help either.

The United States had entered an alliance with many other countries; the World Economic System (W.E.S)." President Asad Bahir Saud of Saudi Arabia was promising gasoline shipments to the countries in need. Inside this organization was also a movement to go to a World Bank, using bitcoin instead of paper money. The U.S. was promising a 'rebate' of sorts, giving a set amount of bitcoin to every family. The internet was mostly working. However, because of our location, a good signal was hard to get. Any little bit of weather would knock it out. Cell phones worked sometimes, again, because of our location. We talked about the need for a land line, but until we could get someone to the farm, we had to make do.

In mid February, the government started a census. They set up stations in every city and you were required to go there, with proper ID, to get your "bank" account set up before you could receive your rebate of bitcoin. Each adult would receive $5000. They took over all the utility companies and those services had not been charged since late October. It was unclear as to whether we would start paying for electricity again.

We discussed how we were going to get into town.

Bill said, "I don't see how we can until we get more gas. I don't think we could make it there and back."

"If there was gas at the stations we could get there and fill up the car," Danny suggested.

"We would have to be sure before we left though," Bill replied.

I had an idea and put it out there, "What if I walked to town and called you when the gas shipment came in?"

"What if it's days before that happens? I don't like the idea of you being on your own in town for that long," Danny interjected.

"I guess you could come with me?" and I smiled at him. "We haven't had a good adventure for a while."

Danny asked, "What does everyone think? That could work."

Bill shook his head, "I don't know, could be risky."

Luke and Jamie both said they didn't like it.

"We could each have a pistol. There are plenty of concealed holsters." I was trying to convince them we would be ok.

Katie said, "That doesn't make me feel any better, John. I think it's too risky!"

We decided to table it for a while and see if our gas shipment came in. We had some time before the deadline.

March came in like a lion, with another big storm. It started with rain, then turned to ice, then to snow, and left a very slippery six inches behind. We were all tired of fighting the winter and Danny snapped at me during chores about not putting the shovel where it belonged and him having to waste time looking for it.

I growled back, "All you had to do was ask me!"

"I shouldn't have to ask you! When you're done, put it away!"

"If I hadn't had to walk over to help Luke with his chores, I would have!"

"I didn't ask you to come help, I could have handled it!" Luke snapped at me.

"Maybe a little less fooling around and a little more work would be nice!" I snapped back at him.

Just then Bill walked in. The three of us just stood there, staring at each other. We didn't say another word, just went back to work. Everyone was silent during the rest of chores, then we trudged back through the snow and ice to the house. We didn't say anything to the girls when we went in, just stomped upstairs to our rooms.

I was tired and angry. My feet were cold and wet, so I changed my socks, knowing I had to go out and chop more wood. I changed out of my barn clothes and went to clean up for lunch. The girls tried talking a little as we ate, but Danny, Luke, and I just stared at our plates.

Finally Bill said, "What's going on?" We looked at each other and shrugged. Megan and Jamie had been working on the horses and had heard the whole argument.

Jamie spoke up, "They were having an argument when you walked in the barn."

"Over what?"

"A shovel."

When Jamie said it like that, it sounded pretty stupid, but I was still mad.

"All right you three, into the living room," Bill commanded.

We glared at each other, but did what Bill said, and we all sat on opposite sides of the room.

He stood in the middle of the room and looked at us, then said, "We're all tired. It's been a long, hard winter, and we've had a lot of life changes. We've had to blend a lot of different personalities in this house. Arguments are going to happen, but we're going to have to learn how to work through them if this is going to work.

The silent treatment is fine while you get your tongues under control, but then you have to talk it out."

We had all been starring at the floor, but when I looked up at Danny, he was looking back at me.

"I'm sorry, John; I shouldn't have snapped at you."

"I'm sorry too," I replied. "I shouldn't have gotten so upset about it. Luke, I'm sorry I yelled at you too. I didn't mean it."

Luke smiled, "All's forgiven."

I looked around the room and everyone was smiling at us. I looked back at Danny and Luke. We walked over to each other and hugged, slapping backs, and shaking hands.

The girls decided we needed some 'fun' time, so planned an afternoon game day. After lunch we were instructed to go to the living room. They had a charades game out on the coffee table.

I stepped back. "I think I need to chop more wood!"

"Oh no you don't, John, you're playing too!" and Janet divided us into two teams. It was me, Bill, Danny, and Katie on one team; Janet, Jamie, Megan, and Luke on the other.

Janet explained the rules. "No talking or mouthing words. If you're asked a question, all you can do is nod yes or no."

Jamie flipped a coin to see who started. Unfortunately, we won.

Danny said, "Katie can go first!"

She drew a card and thought for a moment, then started wiggling her fingers as she moved them from over her head to the floor.

"Rain!" yelled Danny.

She shook her head no and then acted like she was cold, then moved her fingers again. "Snowing!" Bill hollered.

"Yes!" she confirmed, and then sat down.

Luke was excited to go next. He drew a card and smiled. He bent over a little, sticking his butt out, then jumped up quickly. Everyone was laughing.

Janet guessed, "Rabbit!"

He shook his head no, then stuck his butt out again and jumped up quickly.

Jamie yelled, "Frog!"

Luke said no again. This time he bent over and reached his hand out, then jumped up again and put his hands over his butt.

"Pinch!" hollered Megan.

"Yes!" Luke said, putting his finger on his nose.

Danny looked at me, "You go, John!"

I started to object, but Katie said, "You might as well get it over with, John. We're not letting you get out of it!"

Reluctantly, I got up and drew a card. I gave everyone the "What?" look when I read 'disco'.

"Oh . . . this should be good!" Danny laughed.

Bill said, "Just do it!"

I glared and cocked my head. Then I did my best imitation of John Travolta in Saturday Night Fever. Everyone was hysterical, including me! But I kept going, trying to get them to guess.

Katie guessed, "Dancing!"

I gestured, more, and kept going.

Danny hollered, "Disco!"

"Yes!" and I high-fived him.

It felt really good to laugh with everyone; just what we all needed. We finished the game with a lot of crazy antics, laughing, and forgetting about life for a while.

CHAPTER 15

The Census

S LOWLY, March started to promise spring with warmer weather. We still hadn't gotten any gas shipment. The internet was working better with nice weather and we got online to check the status of our gas. It still just said 'pending' with no ETA. I brought up my idea again one evening at dinner about walking into town.

"What if you're there for a few days? Where would you stay? How would you eat? I still don't think it's a good idea," Katie objected.

"We only have 'til the end of April to enroll. The next enrollment isn't until July," I warned. "And since the government is cracking down on the crime, I wouldn't be nervous about leaving the farm."

Bill said, "It would be nice to have some money to buy seed and weed killer for the garden. It will be time to plant again soon. I have some hiking backpacks. What if we packed those up with food for a few days? They could find a secluded place to set up the pup tents and camp for a few nights if they had to."

I looked at Danny, "We could make that work!" He was nodding in agreement.

"I don't want you to stay more than a few days though," Bill warned. "If there's no gas by then, you'll have to walk back home."

Everyone agreed it was worth a try, so we went with Bill to dig the camping equipment out of the attic.

We spent a couple days packing and checking the back packs to be sure we had what we thought we would need. Then on Monday morning we left for town. We figured we could make it in about eight hours if we kept up a good pace. We were both carrying a concealed gun.

"I wonder if we'll see much traffic on the road?" said Danny.

"Look up ahead," I replied, pointing to what looked like a semi truck coming towards us. Each of us just stopped and stared as it went by, like we had never seen a truck before.

"That's got to be a good sign, right?" and Danny slapped me on the back.

There were a few more trucks that went past us as we walked, and it made us hopeful that there would be gas when we got to town, even though what passed us were not fuel trucks.

After about three hours, we stopped for a rest and pulled out our water bottles and some deer sausage sticks. A car was coming down the road, headed towards town, and slowed as it went by. That made both of us nervous. It pulled over and stopped about half a mile ahead of us. We watched as someone got out of the passenger seat. He walked a couple of car lengths towards us, then stopped and waved both arms in the air.

"What do you think that means?" I asked Danny.

"I don't know," and he pulled his gun out of the holster, stuffing it in his pocket.

I did the same.

The guy took a few more steps towards us and waved like he was calling us to him, then pointed to the car.

"Do you think he's trying to give us a ride?" suggested Danny.

"Maybe," I said, standing. "Let's walk towards him."

We put our packs back on and headed towards the car. We stopped maybe 20 feet away.

"You fellas need a ride into town?" the guy shouted. He was African American, maybe in his 30's. "My dad and I are headed there now. There's room in the back seat."

As he was talking, an older man got out of the driver's side and walked towards us.

"We're going there for the census," Danny responded. None of us had moved any closer.

"We're just trying to do the Christian thing, you know, help your neighbor," the guy said with a smile.

Danny and I looked at each other.

"We really appreciate that. My name's Danny and this is John," and Danny walked over to him, extending his hand. I stayed where I was for minute.

"Nice to meet you Danny. I'm Derrick and this is my dad, Darryl," and they all shook hands. I walked over and joined them, shaking hands as well.

"Where are you boys coming from?" Darryl asked, as we walked back to the car.

"We've been staying with friends up the road," I answered. I wasn't sure about sharing too much information with them. "Have you found some open gas stations?"

"That's part of why we're heading to town. What's in this tank is all we have left," Derrick answered.

Danny said, "Us too. We're hoping to call the others when the next shipment comes in so we can fill the car."

On the way into town, we found out Darryl and Derrick lived about 10 miles farther past the farm, in a small, unincorporated town with a population of 75. Well, it used to be 75. They thought there were maybe 40 people left after the rapture, and several of them had left to go stay with other family members. The 10 people who remained pooled their resources so they could make it through the winter.

As we drove into town, Darryl pointed out the factory where they used to work. When we got to the gas station, there was a sign that said, "Next shipment Tuesday." He pulled in and parked.

Derrick looked at him and said, "I guess we'll camp in the car till then."

"Do you know where the census building is?" I asked as I gathered my gear.

Derrick answered, "Yes, we can walk there with you. Dad, let's leave the car here so we don't use anymore gas, ok?"

Darryl nodded in agreement, and we all got out.

"The census is at the courthouse. It's up on the square about six blocks," and Derrick led the way.

There was a pretty long line that wrapped around the block when we got there, so we found the end and set our backpacks down while we waited. I pulled out four more deer sausage sticks and passed them out to everyone.

"Thank you!" Darryl said. "We didn't have much food left to pack."

This was the first time I noticed how thin they looked. I looked down the line. Everyone looked pretty thin.

The line moved pretty slowly. Darryl was softly humming something, and then Danny was humming along. I recognized it as one of the hymns Danny played sometimes in our Sunday morning 'church' services. "Jesus saves, Jesus saves," they softly harmonized. Someone behind us scowled at them, either not appreciating their singing ability, or the message.

We finally got to the front of the line where we were handed four pages of documents to fill out. They wanted current address and previous address, social security number, DOB, sex, ethnicity, phone number, immediate family that was still living, emergency contact, old bank information with account numbers, drivers license, occupation, and religion. They also wanted your concealed carry information and asked if you had guns, wanting you to list them. I put down my concealed carry information, but did not put that I owned any guns. Technically, I didn't own them. When I had finished, I handed them to a gentleman who looked them over.

"You didn't put any family members down."

"I don't think I have any family left here."

"You don't 'think'? You're not sure?"

"I haven't spoken to my father in over 10 years. He would be the only one."

"And what was his name?"

"Jack Blakely."

He wrote that down. "I see you have a concealed carry, but you didn't list any guns?"

"No. I had one several years ago, but sold it. I sent in all the proper forms; it should be on file somewhere."

He made a few more notes, then sent me to the next station with another piece of paper. This was where you got your new bank card. After presenting my ID, and confirming my name, address, and social security number, I received what looked like a debit card. I had to sign the back in front of a witness, and they stamped it, explaining how it worked just like the old debit, but used bitcoin instead of cash. I was to go online to set up and activate my account. Once activated, the $5000.00 would be deposited within three business days.

As I waited for Danny to finish, I heard a lot of shouting coming from outside the building and stepped out to see what was happening. There was a large crowd encircling someone, shouting something at them. I couldn't see who it was until someone shoved a guy down and the crowd parted a bit. It was Darryl! Derrick was trying to help him up when someone shoved him too. I ran over to the crowd, pushing my way through.

"What's going on?!" I yelled, trying to push them back.

"We don't need that self righteous judgement!" someone yelled.

"You Christians think you're so much better; you're just a bunch of hypocrites!" another in the crowd yelled. They kept pressing in on us, shoving and pushing.

Darryl was shouting, "You don't understand! It's not too late! You can still be saved!"

I grabbed Darryl's arm and tried to drag him through the mob. Derrick was on his other arm. The crowd did not move easily, and we had to push people out of the way.

I felt a spray of something on my head, and realized they were throwing small rocks at us from the landscaping. I kept pulling Darryl, trying to get as far away as possible, when Danny showed up. He could see the angry mob. "What happened?"

I just shook my head and kept walking. When we had gotten a few blocks away we stopped.

"How did that start?" I asked, looking at Darryl.

"I was just trying to tell them what happened, that it was the last chance to get right with God, but they didn't want to hear it. They'd rather believe everything the government is saying."

Derrick looked at him and said, "Dad, you've got to be careful who you talk to! The world is a different place now, people are dangerous!"

"I know son, but they need to know."

Derrick gave him a hug and we walked back to the gas station with them.

Once back at the gas station we asked the owner if the shipment was still coming Tuesday. He said it was, as far as he knew, and that it usually came early.

"Do you have someplace I can charge my phone?" I asked him.

He took me over to an outside outlet on the corner of the building and said I could use that.

"Thanks!" Danny and I both got our chargers out and plugged in our phones.

He stayed outside with us, so I struck up a conversation. "Are you the owner?"

"Yes" he responded. Then added "I used to be, anyway." He looked at us, then went on, "Everything belongs to the government now. They've let all the business owners know who was allowed to open back up." He lit up a cigarette. "It's not all bad; I don't have a mortgage anymore." He took another long drag. "And I get first crack at the supplies!" He smiled, holding up the cigarette.

"Are you still taking cash?" Danny asked him.

"Yes. Until the end of the registration period. Then you will have to use your card. There's not much cash left out there though."

"What are they charging for gas?" I asked him.

"I don't know till it gets here, but last time it was $10.00 a gallon. The W.E.S. sets the price." He threw down his cigarette and ground it under his shoe. "They're pretty much in charge of every-thing now." And he went back into the store.

I tried calling Bill, and he answered. I told him we were fine and about the shipment expected early tomorrow.

"Ok, I'll come with Janet in the morning to get gas and regis-ter. Then we'll have to send the other four after we get back." We planned to meet at the station at first light.

The next morning, we were at the station at the crack of dawn. There were already a few cars in line at the pump. We hadn't been there long when Bill and Janet pulled up. They got in the line and we hopped in the back seat. The morning was chilly, and we were thankful for the warm car. Janet handed back a thermos of coffee and two cups. "You are a life saver!" I said to her, taking the thermos. I had told Bill to bring what money he had, in case our accounts were not activated by the time the gas came in. We told them about Darryl and Derrick giving us a ride to town and about the scene at the courthouse. They were the first car in line at the pump.

I told Bill about the paperwork at the courthouse and that they were asking for a list of all guns.

Bill said, "I inherited all those guns from my grandfather and father. I don't think I'll put any of them on the paper. I don't trust them. The W.E.S. has taken over everything."

We sat there till nine, when the census opened, and then Bill and Janet left us the cash and walked over to get registered while Danny and I stayed in the gas line. The truck finally pulled in at 11:00am and by 11:30 we started pumping gas. Neither of our accounts were activated so we had to use the cash. There was $230.00 and we pumped in $180.00 worth of gas, filling the tank. As we pulled out of the station we saw Janet and Bill walking up the street, so we went to pick them up.

"How did it go?" Danny asked as they got in the back seat.

"Pretty good. They were very interested in the farm and asked if I was going to plant crops this spring. I told them we would need to have gas delivered to the farm to run the tractors. They made some notes . . . maybe we'll get bumped up the list." Then Bill said, "Let's get home so the others can make it before they close."

CHAPTER 16

The Storm

T HE spring weather was upon us, with lots of rain and storms. One morning a loud crack of thunder woke me up before my alarm. I got up and got ready for chores, then went downstairs. Bill and Janet were already down there and she handed me some coffee with a smile and a "good morning!" They were trying to check the weather radar, but the clouds were thick and it wasn't working.

"We could be in for some severe weather today," Bill said.

Katie came in just as another loud crack shook the house. "That will wake you up quick!" she said as she jumped a little. "Sounds like it is right over the top of us!"

By the time we finished breakfast the rain had let up a little, so we hurried to the barn. About an hour into chores, we could hear another storm approaching. The horses were getting spooked as the thunder got louder, and Megan and Jamie were trying to calm them down. We could hear the wind blowing things around and I went over to the door to see what it was. The trash bin came flying across the yard and slammed into the side of the barn. Just then I saw Katie come running out of the house towards us. She was yelling something, but the storm drowned out her sound. She was motioning towards the back of the house when a large tree came crashing down right on top of her! I yelled for the others and went running out to her . . . that's when I saw it. A tornado was forming over the top of the trees just behind the house. I reached Katie first but couldn't move the tree. Then the others were all there trying to move it, but fighting the wind and rain, we could not budge it. We all saw the tornado coming and I waved them all to head to the cellar. They kept trying to move the tree, but it was useless. Finally, Bill pushed everyone towards the house, and they ran for the cellar, barely able to keep their footing in the wind. He tried to pull me into the house with him but I couldn't leave her, so I shoved him towards the house and got down on the ground, trying to cover Katie with my body to protect her. I grabbed hold of a large branch and hung on as the tornado moved over the top of us. I could feel debris and hail pelting my back . . . and then it was over. When I looked up part of the roof was blown off and trees were scattered across the yard. I checked Katie . . . she was conscious but having trouble breathing from the weight of the tree. I could see the fear in her eyes as I struggled again, trying to free her, but could not move it. Everyone was pouring out of the house, running over to help. We all grabbed the trunk, and together were able to lift it.

Jamie hollered, "I'll let go and pull her out, everyone hang on!" We strained under the weight of it but held on till she was clear.

"On three drop it!" yelled Bill. "One, two, three!" and we all let go.

Everyone surrounded Katie. Jamie was already down at her head, trying to calm her. Bill was trying to check her injuries and feeling for her pulse. She was still laboring to breath and when we tried to move her, she screamed in pain, so we stopped. I looked at Bill for instructions, but he only shook his head.

Jamie said, "John, I think she wants to tell you something," and he stood up. I got down on the ground right next to her head and she took my hand.

"You're going to be ok. We'll get you to the hospital," I choked out.

She shook her head a little and put her hand over my mouth. "It's ok. I'm not scared," she said in short gasps. "Thank you . . . " she started, but I tried to stop her.

"Don't talk," I said. "Save your breath."

She covered my mouth again and smiled at me. "My knight in shining armor." Her breath was easier now. "I'll see you on the other side . . . " Her hand fell.

"Katie . . . Katie!" I tried shaking her, but Danny pulled me off. I backed up in disbelief as Bill checked her and then stood up, staring at Janet. She fell into his arms, crying. Jamie was holding Megan as she silently wept. I stood there, looking from Danny to Luke, like they had some kind of answer for me. Danny walked over to me and tried to hug me, but I tried to walk away. He wouldn't let me . . . He grabbed me and wouldn't let go, and I started to weep in his arms. Luke walked into the house and came out with a big quilt, the one that Katie had on her bed, the one she had admired, and laid it over her. We all helped wrap her in the warm blanket and carried her into the barn, laying her in some fresh hay. One by one we walked out of the barn, each one touching the blanket before they left, until I was the only one still there. I laid my hand on her and with tears still rolling down my face, thanked God that He had brought her into my life. "I'll see you on the other side."

We were all standing outside of the barn, taking in the scene before us. The house had lost part of its roof, but otherwise looked ok. There were several downed trees and branches scattered around the yard. The barns and chicken coop looked untouched. Bill said, "Someone want to help me get the big tarps out of the machine barn?" All the men went with him. Janet and Megan started picking up the roofing debris and piling it next to the house. There was very little talking. We were all trying to process what had just happened, but there was no time to waste. We had to get the roof covered before more rain came.

The five men all climbed up on the roof with two large tarps. The damage could have been much worse—it seemed that only the shingles had blown off; the wood still looked good. As we spread the tarp Luke started to slip on the wet shingles and scared everyone to death. Bill was closest to him and grabbed his shirt, stopping the slide. There was a collective sigh as we all started to breathe again. When the tarp was secured, we started cleaning up the yard with Janet and Megan. The car had gas, but the chain saw did not, so we left the downed trees for another time.

Bill and Janet walked back into the house and a few minutes later Bill called out the door for all of us to come in. We gathered in the living room.

Janet started to say, "We want to bury Katie . . . " but she couldn't finish, so Bill took over.

"We want to bury Katie out in the family cemetery, if that's ok with all of you."

No one could talk, we just nodded in agreement.

That evening everyone was pretty quiet. I went upstairs early and just sat on my bed for a while. Words just didn't come to me, but I felt like I needed to talk. I was sure Katie was with the Lord in heaven, and took comfort in that, but still had this emptiness inside. As I got ready for bed, my eyes locked on the small figure of the horse and knight that she had given me for Christmas sitting on my dresser. I picked it up gently and placed it in my top drawer, covering it with clothes. A knight in shining armor saves the girl . . .

At first light we gathered at the little cemetery by the edge of the woods with shovels and picks, and everyone took turns digging. Then we walked to the barn and gently carried Katie to the grave and laid her in it.

Danny read a passage from Romans 8: "Who will separate us from the love of Christ? Will hardship, or distress, or persecution, or famine, or nakedness, or peril, or sword? No, in all these things we are more than conquerors through him who loved us.

For I am convinced that neither death, nor life, nor angels, nor rulers, nor things present, nor things to come, nor powers, nor height, nor depth, nor anything else in all creation, will be able to separate us from the love of God in Christ Jesus our Lord."

He went on, "Katie, I'm going to miss your laugh at the dinner table, your kind heart and your spunk. Say hi to Elle for me. Tell her I'm coming."

"Katie, you were like the daughter I never had," Janet started, then swallowed hard. "I loved getting to know you. I'm going to miss you by my side in the kitchen. Save me a place at the table."

We quietly stood there a few more minutes and then picked up the shovels. Silent tears rolled down everyone's face as we covered her over with dirt.

Later that morning, while we were still in the barn, a car pulled in the driveway. We all got a little nervous until Danny and I recognized Darryl and Derrick as they got out of the car.

"We wanted to be sure you were all ok after the storm," Darryl said, walking over to us.

We shook hands and introduced them to everyone. "Looks like you came out ok, just some roof and tree damage," Derrick observed.

I looked at Danny, not knowing what to say. Then he explained what had happened with Katie to them.

They both said they were sorry, and started to leave, but Bill and Janet insisted that they stay for lunch. We wouldn't take no for an answer, so they finally agreed.

During lunch we learned that Derrick's stepmom had been raptured. That they both had never given much thought to Jesus, but afterward had believed the gospel message of salvation through Christ, and had witnessed to the remaining people, and how they started to help each other. They would get together every morning in the small church and read from the Word, discussing everyone's needs. They broke into the homes that were empty, using whatever supplies there were, promising to pay them back should they return (much like Katie and I had done at the store).

Darryl said they had a chain saw and some gas in a can that they could bring over, so after lunch they went home to get it and came back. We used the chain saws to cut through the biggest pieces and the axe on the rest. While we worked, they invited us to the Sunday services they were starting. Darryl wanted to get the word out to any believers that they could come and worship with them. After the yard was cleared they said they better get back home. We thanked them for their help, saying we would try to come for a service, and they left.

CHAPTER 17

The Church

I T was about a month later when we made a Sunday morning drive to the small town where Darryl and Derrick lived. The gas tank on the farm had been filled, so we piled in the van. On the ride over, the memory of Katie in our first van ride played in my head.

When we got there, Derrick greeted us in the parking lot. "Welcome! Thank you for coming!" We all shook hands and he walked us into the church. I was surprised at the number of people there, counting about 30. They were getting ready to start, so we took a seat in an empty pew. An attractive young woman sat down at the piano and started playing. I looked at Danny and he mouthed "wow" at me as she played flawlessly. As I sat there, I realized this was the first real 'church service' I had been to. The music was peppy and the singing loud and cheerful. People were raising their hands in praise. Then Darryl got up and gave an inspiring message from the Bible.

When it was over, I went up to him, shaking his hand, saying "You sound like a real preacher!" He laughed. "I meant that as a compliment," I said, winking at him. He asked how the farm was doing and we talked a bit. When someone else got his attention, I looked around for the others. Danny was standing by the piano talking to the girl that had played for church. Luke was near him talking with a small group of people. Everyone was very friendly and I think we spoke with all of them before we left. On the way home it seemed like everyone was in a good mood. It felt so good to have some outside contact with people—these people anyway.

We continued to go to church services as often as possible. Danny and Danisha, the piano player, would sit at the piano after every service and she would try to show him how to play like she did. Luke, Jamie, and Megan had fit right in with the other group of twenty something's. We were a pretty diverse group; black, white, brown, mixed, from 18 to 60's, it didn't matter. There was a genuine caring for each other. If someone had a need, we all did what we could to help.

Chapter 18

The Fire

WHILE our little group was getting along nicely, the rest of the world was not. The W.E.S. was seizing control of everything, with little resistance, if any, from the various countries. It reminded me of the Nazi regimes as they demanded people pledge their allegiance. Small groups that did resist were being gunned down or arrested. So far, they had left us alone, and we hoped it would stay that way.

Bill was told what crops he could plant and he didn't argue. He and Jamie drove the big equipment and the rest of us did what we could to help. Mostly we took over the chores while they planted.

Extreme weather had become the norm with many violent storms. Every week it seemed we were in the cellar praying no damage would come to the house and barns. Volcanoes were erupting in every country and the earth shook with quakes often.

One evening at dinner Jamie and Megan made an announcement. "We want to get married," they said in unison. I wasn't really surprised, but wondered if it was the smart thing to do. One thing we knew for sure, whatever life we had left was not going to be easy. When no one spoke up right away Jamie went on, "Look, we know that things are bad, and getting worse. None of us know how much time we have left on this earth; whether we will make it to the end alive or not. But Megan and I love each other, and whatever that looks like, we want to be together."

Janet said, "This would not be a good place to bring up a child, have you thought of that?"

"I got an IUD from Planned Parenthood just after we moved here," Megan said, looking at Jamie. He squeezed her hand.

"We'd like to have Darryl marry us in his church," Jamie went on.

We all looked at each other, and then Janet went over and gave them both a big hug. "You should be happy as long as you can. Megan, I have my wedding dress up in the attic. We can see if it fits you if you want to wear it."

"I'd love that!" Megan replied, and they disappeared up the stairs.

Bill went over to Jamie and shook his hand, "Congratulations!"

I did the same, "I'm really happy for you!"

"Is it ok if we stay here with you?" Jamie asked Bill.

"Of course! I wouldn't want it any other way." And Bill gave him a hug.

They talked to Darryl and he said he would love to marry them. The date was set for mid-June and Janet and Megan worked behind closed doors on the dress.

The date came quickly and everyone from the church came. They had put up some candelabras and other wedding decorations. Danisha played the piano and Danny sang a song they had requested. Megan looked beautiful as she walked down the aisle in Janet's dress with Bill by her side. I really was happy for them, but a little jealous too. Men won't admit it, but we think about this day too . . . a family of our own. For a wedding present all of us had secretly worked on one of the empty houses near the church and turned it into their 'honeymoon' suite. I'm sure the tiny town of Greenville was not what Megan had dreamed of for her honeymoon, but it was the best we could do, and they were both thrilled when we showed it to them. We had stocked it with two weeks of food and Bill said then they "needed to get back home and help," laughing and winking.

Spring started out wet, but by the end of July we were in a drought. There were a lot of springs on Bill's land with creeks and small ponds. His well had never run dry and we used it to water the garden. We used the ponds to fill the water tanks for the irrigation system to keep the soybeans alive. The temperature was averaging in the upper 90's with some days over 120 degrees. We put a 'tent' of sorts over the garden and covered the plants in the hottest part of the day. It was yielding a good crop, despite the weather, and we all learned how to can.

We made occasional trips into town to pick up staples like flour, sugar, and paper products. It was a celebration when we found toilet paper on the shelves! You never knew what you would run into though. People had become angry and desperate. Tolerance for anyone thinking differently than you was all but gone, so we were very careful not to engage in strangers' conversations. Darryl was not good at that and would still try to witness to people. Derrick told us of a near riot breaking out in the grocery store one day after his dad had tried inviting some people to church. He said they barely escaped without bodily harm.

Mid-September we starting harvesting the fields of soybeans. We were still in a drought and all the grass was dry and dead, but we had managed to save some of the crop. Bill was instructed where to take the truck loads of beans and there was a small payment made to his bitcoin account. He shook his head saying even with a bad year he could have made four times that amount a year ago. There was a no burn notice nationwide and when fires did break out, they were mostly uncontrollable. We hadn't burned anything outside since August. Our well still had a good amount of water, though Bill said it was lower than he had ever seen it.

Sunday morning Danny, Jamie, Megan, and Janet took the small car early to help with the services. Danny was going to play with Danisha, and Jamie, Megan, and Janet were helping fix some of the pews and window curtains. Jamie was doing some woodwork on them and Megan and Janet were meeting some other women there to sew up some tears in the fabric. The rest of us stayed back to take care of the livestock before we left. Once finished, we piled in the old truck and drove the 10 miles to church to meet the others. We finished singing and Darryl was just getting up to preach when someone yelled, "The yard is on fire!" Everyone ran to the windows and doors to look out. I was at the front door and saw a pickup truck spin its wheels, peeling out of the driveway, headed towards town. Derrick was yelling for everyone to get out of the building.

Someone else had grabbed an old fire extinguisher and was trying to put the fire out but it was already spreading to all the nearby homes. Everyone was running towards their houses and many grabbed their garden hoses, trying to water down the grass to keep the fire away. Others were dragging belongings out of their homes and piling them into cars hoping to make an escape and salvage something. I ran to one of the houses and grabbed the hose, turning it on and spraying down the grass and house. Because there were so many hoses going the water pressure was nearly gone. Danny was hollering for the nearest houses to use the hoses and the rest to turn them off to try to get more pressure, but no one listened. Everyone was panicking and cars were speeding out of the parking lot.

My heart sank as I watched the church start to burn. The fire was hot and climbing the trees and bushes, racing across the dry grass towards all the homes. The garden hoses did not deliver enough water to stop it. I started running into homes, helping people get out what they could and throwing it into cars. The vehicles that were parked near grassy areas were catching fire. Luke drove our little truck over and we started pulling all the food and supplies we could get from each home and threw them in the back. We were screaming at everyone to get out. The homes were starting to burn and there was no stopping it now. Danny ran over to Danisha's house, helping her get out what she could, then told her she had to go, now! She got in her car and picked up some neighbors that did not have a car, and they drove out through the flames, heading towards town.

Bill grabbed Janet and Megan and pushed them in our car, then told Jamie to drive them out, that he would be right behind them with us in the truck. Danny and I were going door to door to make sure everyone was out and Luke and Bill joined us. Some of the homes were fully engulfed by now and the church roof was caving in.

I watched Danny and Luke enter a home across the street as I was coming out of one. Suddenly there was an explosion and the home they were in burst into flames. I ran over there, kicking the door in and the flames shot out at me. Bill pulled up with the truck yelling we needed to get out! I ran to the truck, grabbing a blanket, and shouted, "Danny and Luke are in there!" He jumped out of the truck, also grabbing a blanket and we both ran back to the house. We laid the blanket against the door to tamp down the fire so we could go through it. The heat was so intense I could feel my arm hair singe. We got into the house, yelling for them, and then I saw Luke in the back. He was trying to free Danny, who's leg was trapped under a fallen beam. We made our way over and used one blanket to tamp down a small fire near him. Then we all tried pushing the beam off, but it was wedged by something. It looked like some of the wall had fallen in on it.

I went over to the wall and started smashing it with some debris, trying to loosen its grip on Danny, while Bill and Luke kept trying to lift it off. We still couldn't budge it. There was another large beam that I grabbed, and we wedged it under the one trapping Danny, using it like a fulcrum to lift it, but when it started to raise the wall started to collapse even more. I yelled for Bill and Luke to keep pushing it up so Danny could get out, that I would hold the wall up. I pushed my back into the hot wall, bracing myself against the door jam with my legs. I motioned for them to lift it and get him out. They both pushed with everything they had and lifted it enough that Danny could pull himself free, then grabbed him and started to carry him out.

Luke looked back at me and I motioned for them to go. I didn't know how I was going to let the wall go with out it crashing down on me, but I wanted to be sure they got him out before I tried. After they cleared the door, I let up on the pressure a bit and could feel the whole thing sagging down on me. I pushed back hard, trying to stop the collapse, and it held for a few seconds. Thoughts of Elle and Katie flooded my brain. Pictures of the farm, of Danny saving me, of Bill and Janet, Jamie and Megan, of Luke. I had no strength left and could barely breath in the smoke and flames. "Thank you for this family, watch over them." And I let go . . . of all the struggles I had ever had.

One month later.

Danny was going through John's dresser, to see if there were some clothes in there that Derrick could wear. After the fire he and Darryl had moved onto the farm, along with Danisha and Jill, one of her friends. They had lost everything in the fires and Bill and Janet, everyone really, had insisted they move in. There were two empty bedrooms since they lost Katie and John.

Danny found the small sculpture wrapped in a shirt and took it downstairs. He remembered the night of the fire, how John had given his life to save him. How they had tried to go back in to get him but the flames engulfed the building, and shortly after, the walls collapsed. How they had gone back after the fires burned out, to see if they could find some remains to bury in the graveyard next to Katie. He held up the figure to show everyone and they all stopped to remember. "I found it tucked in his drawer, hidden in a shirt."

Janet took the figure from Danny and cleared a spot on the fireplace mantle for it.

Danisha asked what it was and Danny went back to the beginning, telling her the story of John.

Revelation 7:13-17 ESV

Then one of the elders addressed me, saying, "Who are these, clothed in white robes, and from where have they come?"

I said to him, "Sir, you know."

And he said to me, "These are the ones coming out of the great tribulation. They have washed their robes and made them white in the blood of the Lamb.

Therefore they are before the throne of God, and serve Him day and night in his temple; and He who sits on the throne will shelter them with His presence.

They shall hunger no more, neither thirst anymore; the sun shall not strike them, nor any scorching heat.

For the Lamb in the midst of the throne will be their shepherd, and He will guide them to springs of living water, and God will wipe away every tear from their eyes."

Made in the USA
Monee, IL
28 November 2022

18791488R00075